15

THE COTTAGE AT BANTRY BAY

By the Same Author

The Cottage at Bantry Bay

WRITTEN AND ILLUSTRATED BY

Hilda van Stockum

BETHLEHEM BOOKS • IGNATIUS PRESS

WARSAW, N.D.   SAN FRANCISCO

Originally published by
The Viking Press

Text and illustrations © 1938 by Hilda van Stockum
Copyright renewed 1966 by the author

Special features
© 1995 Bethlehem Books

Second Printing: 1997

ISBN 1-883937-06-X
Library of Congress Catalog Number: 96-78060

Cover art by Hilda van Stockum
Cover design by Davin Carlson

Bethlehem Books • Ignatius Press
15605 County Road 15
Minto, ND 58261
Printed in the United States of America

To My Mother,

Who Minded the Babies

Contents

Full Page Illustrations

FULL PAGE ILLUSTRATIONS

THE COTTAGE AT BANTRY BAY

Father O'Sullivan

ONE

Father Tells a Story

BRIGID sat in the corner of the big kitchen, trying to put a patch in one of Liam's breeches. She had to help her mother as much as she could, for Mrs. O'Sullivan had her hands full with the washing and cleaning, and the feeding of the men folk, not forgetting the chickens and pigs and the cabbage patch. Father was out all the time in wind and weather; he did the rough work, the haying and the plowing, the fishing and the cutting of turf. There was little he could not do, from mending Mother's pots and pans and broken furniture to slaughtering pigs and playing the pipes. But he would leave odds and ends scattered about the place and Mother was forever tidying after him. Brigid sighed. She had no liking for needlework; she would rather have been a big boy like Michael, able to help his father shoot rabbits. "Ow!" she cried as the needle stuck in her thumb and the blood pearled up like a round, red jewel. Brigid sucked the sore spot and watched Mother, who was putting plates on the scrubbed deal table for tea. It would soon be time for Father to come home, and then she could stop sewing.

The black kettle, hung on the chain over the fire, sang softly as Mother moved about, cutting the bread and putting scant butter on each slice. Then she kneaded something in a bowl and flattened it out on the table, fashioning nice round slabs.

"Oh, is it potato cakes you're making, Mother?" cried Brigid, sitting straight with sudden interest.

Mother smiled. "It is so bad a day, there was need for something to fill ye all," she said.

Indeed it was bad weather. The rain had been beating against the windowpanes all day long, and dark clouds chased over the mountain tops.

Mother put the cakes into a skillet and crouched in front of the fire, turning them quickly with a fork. A

Mother O'Sullivan

Brigid

delicious smell of fried butter filled the kitchen. Suddenly Mother stopped and turned around.

"I haven't heard the twins this long time," she said. "Do you know where they are?"

Brigid gladly put down the breeches and jumped up. "They're sure to be out in the rain," she said. "Shall I fetch them in?"

"Do so. Francie's so delicate he might catch his death of cold."

Brigid threw a shawl over her head and slipped out of the back door. She looked all over the yard, the mud squeezing between her bare toes, and called: "Francie! Liam!" but there was no answer. The chickens left their shelter and ran to her, hoping with greedy little eyes that she would throw them some food. But she was intent on finding the boys and called again, cupping her hands around her mouth: "Francie and Liam!"

The blue Kerry mountains, looming behind the green fields, threw the sound back at her; still there were no answering shouts from the twins. She went around the whitewashed cottage and peeped down the road. The cottage stood halfway up a hill; below she could see several thatched roofs, with turf smoke curling from the chimneys. Through the trees there were silver glimpses of Bantry Bay. But it was not at the scenery Brigid gazed;

Francie

Liam

there was something else to attract her attention. For, in the middle of the road, where horses' hoofs had pawed a groove which the rain was transforming into a river, two little boys stood ankle deep in the water, spattered with mud from grimy legs to sopping hair. They were scooping up the dirt with some old battered cans, and they hailed her gladly.

"Come and see, Biddy. Come and see!" cried Francie, dancing up and down in his excitement. "We've built a bridge that'll keep the enemy out of the country entirely.

Liam is the Sassenach and I'm a Sinn Feiner. When he comes with his men I'll knock them all into the river...." He brandished a stick.

Liam seemed less happy. "I'm no Sassenach," he kept repeating. "I'm a patriot." But Francie would not listen.

"Come and see, Biddy," he repeated. "It's the grandest bridge ever you saw, and I've me fleet ready!" He pointed to an empty matchbox which was floating uncertainly in the puddle. But Brigid did not admire.

"Shame on ye!" she cried. "It's kilt ye'll be, with the damp and the dirt. Come along in now, or Mother'll be after ye!"

"You're always spoiling the game!" Francie grumbled indignantly. "It's a real woman ye are an' no mistake."

Liam was more lenient. "Sure, she means no harm," he said protectively. "Come, Francie."

"Wait a minute." Francie rescued his matchbox, wiping it carefully and stuffing it into one of his pockets, the one without a hole. He threw one last rueful glance at his lovely bridge and, as he did so, saw something else which made him cry out.

Brigid and Liam turned around and repeated his cry.

"Father! What's after happening to him?" It was a sorry pair they saw stumbling up the road, Michael supporting his father, who seemed scarcely able to walk.

Michael

Brigid flew to meet them, Liam at her heels, and Francie last, for the poor lad had a crippled foot. Michael hailed them from afar and tried to tell them what had happened, but there was no making it out until they had come closer. It appeared that Father had stumbled into a rabbit hole and twisted his ankle so that he could hardly walk. Michael had had some trouble getting him on his feet again and down the treacherous mountainside. Once on the road, it had been easier, although Father had been forced to rest ever so often and had suffered great pain. His ankle was badly swollen.

"The rabbits got meself this time," he said, with a faint smile; Michael had to do the rest of the explaining because Father was too busy stifling his groans.

Brigid offered to support him on the other side and between her and Michael the poor man was brought safely home. The twins ran ahead to tell Mother, who came to meet Father with outstretched arms.

Father was soon settled in a comfortable chair by the fire, his sprained foot on a stool. Mother bathed his ankle many times in hot water till he began to feel a little better and was able to eat some potato cakes and drink a cup of tea. What with the excitement and bustle Mother had paid no attention to the twins. Now she noticed their appearance as they stood eating their cakes with grimy hands, the gray mud slowly drying in patches on their faces and clothes.

"Mercy on us!" she said, staring. "Is there any dirt left outside at all, at all?"

After that she had no peace until the little boys were thoroughly scrubbed and cleaned—even their ears got a turn, much to Francie's disgust. Then the two were allowed to sit near the fire to dry and had to drink hot tea to keep colds away.

Mother washed up the tea things and settled herself in a chair with her knitting. Michael fetched Father's pipe and tobacco and took a stool to sit beside him, whilst Brigid and her homemade rag doll shared the bench in the chimney corner with the twins. They made a nice picture, as they sat around the flickering fire. Michael, the eldest boy, had a round freckled face, merry blue eyes, and a mop of red hair; Brigid was the pretty one with red-gold curls and an elfin face. The chubby twins looked like sweet blond cherubs, though they often acted otherwise.

"How are ye feeling now, Father?" Mrs. O'Sullivan asked anxiously, when she had finished counting stitches.

"Better, much better," Father said. "But I'm afraid I won't be able to go to Kenmare tomorrow to bring Farmer Flynn the donkey he wanted to buy from me."

"Will he mind, Father?" Michael asked.

11

Father smiled sadly. "He may not, son-o, but *I* do. He may buy some other donkey, and then where will we be? Mother needs the money, doesn't she?"

Mother sighed a little, but she smiled bravely and said: "No harm, we'll manage." By the way her needles clicked the children could tell she did mind. There was always a lot to be bought and never much money to do it with. Though Mother did turn around clothes till they looked like new and managed to use every scrap of food to great advantage, Michael and Brigid knew full well there was need of money always. Never had there been enough to buy Bridy a proper doll, and she did so long for one. For though the doll she had was fondly cherished, it had no face. One misses a face. Brigid wanted a doll with blue eyes and a red mouth full of pearly teeth. She had seen several in the shop windows when Father took her to town on market days, but she was afraid she would never have one. She was now nine years old; when you were twelve, you were too old to play with dolls. What a pity it would be, thought Brigid, if she had to grow up without ever having a real doll! She sighed a little as she thought of it. Grownup people led such dull lives. It was a wonder they got through the days. They were always mending and working and worrying. Of course, she would have to grow up sometime, but she'd like to enjoy herself first, and then, when the mysterious thing happened and she had to let down her skirts and put up her hair, she would at least have something to look back on. But she was afraid there never would be enough money, and so she gazed sadly at the faceless creature on her lap. There were other things that could not be had because they cost money. There was the cow Father had set his heart on, the Sunday hat Mother needed, and Michael wanted to go to a good school, for he was clever and the village teacher said he was getting too knowing for her. Money was needed most for poor Francie, who had a club-foot and could not walk well. The doctor who had seen him said there was a hospital in Dublin where he would be treated free of charge, but Dublin was a long way off, and it would cost so much to get him there.

"Couldn't I sell the donkey for you, Father?" Michael asked.

"It's too far, me lad," said his father, but he looked as though it was not such a bad idea.

"It's not so far. Many's the day I've walked further than that. I'm sure I can do it!"

"Oh, I wish you'd take me with you!" cried Brigid. "I'd love to go!"

Mother sat frowning; presently she looked up and said: "It may be a good plan, Father, to let both of them go.

13

They're fine healthy children, God bless their hearts, and if one of them is in trouble the other can let us know. I'd sooner they went together. It's safer I think, and we're in sore need of the money."

Father stroked his chin, looking doubtful. "It's a deal of money to carry all that way, boy-o," he said. "Are ye able for it, Micky? Can I be trusting you to bring it to me and not to lose it foolishly on the road?"

"Oh, Father, you can surely! I was eleven last Easter."

"Faith and that's true," said Father with a little chuckle. "Your age frightens me." And he put his hand caressingly on the boy's head. "Maybe now you are able to do it, but will it be too much for Biddy?"

"Oh, no, Father!" cried Biddy. "We can be riding the donkey one way and walk back!"

"Well," said Father, pulling at his pipe, "it will ease my mind if you can sell the creature. He is eating all my grass and sorra a bit of work he does."

"Oh! Won't it be the grand journey, Michael?" cried Brigid excitedly. "Isn't it through the tunnel we go?"

"We do, and we'll see the fine new bridge over Kenmare River. . . ."

The word "bridge" woke up Francie, who had been dozing on his bench. "It's meself had the fine bridge," he

14

said with an angry glance at Brigid. "But women will never leave a man alone."

"What's that?" Father asked, and Brigid had to explain Francie's game.

"And I was to be a Sassenach!" Liam cried indignantly. "An O'Sullivan can't be a Sassenach, can he now, Father?"

"But you wouldn't be an O'Sullivan then," said Francie. "It's somebody else you'd be entirely. You wouldn't even know yourself."

Liam looked as though this was small consolation. He was ready to burst into tears, when the thought of his noble O'Sullivan blood restrained him.

"Will you pass the Eagles' Nest tomorrow, Michael?" Francie asked.

"We will then, we'll pass all the high mountain peaks and go right into Kerry. It will be a proud journey."

"Oh, Father," coaxed Liam. "Tell us the story of the Eagles' Nest again. I do want to hear it, and you said you were going to tell us a story if we were good. We have been powerful good, haven't we, Francie?"

"I have," said Francie, virtuously.

"Don't let them bother you, Father, if your foot hurts," Mother warned. "Just take it easy."

But Father said that what with the flickering of flames

15

in the hearth and the rustling of rain on the roof he could not be in a better mood for telling a tale. He filled his pipe anew, and Brigid put some more turf on the grate. Let the winds howl outside; they were going to have a grand time, for Father was the best story-teller in County Cork. Father blew a big cloud of smoke up the chimney, looked at the firelit faces of his four children, and began:

"Ye know that this country was not always a free state. Years and years ago it was independent and was governed by a high king, called *Ard-ri*. Then the English came with their fine armor and hired soldiers, and the Irish had to put up a fight for seven hundred and fifty years to win their freedom."

"Seven hundred and fifty years!" cried Liam. "Sure an' weren't some of 'em tired fighting that long!"

"Och," said Francie. "Little ye know. Irishmen never get tired of fighting, do they now, Father?"

"They do then, son-o! The story I am going to tell happened when they were weary of it, indeed. The war of Munster had been going on for a long time, and the Irish warriors were half starved, for the crops had failed, and the people were crawling in ditches to eat the greens!"

"Raw?" asked Brigid.

"Raw, indeed," said Father. "They weren't particular. So when our ancestor, the great O'Sullivan who owned a

16

castle on Bantry Bay, was driven out by the English, he took his cattle with him to have something to eat whilst he hid in the woods with his men and his wife and children.

"But och! The English were too wise for him; they pursued him and robbed all his cattle.

"Now the great O'Sullivan and his people seemed lost entirely, the way they were left in the deep dark woods with ne'er a bite to eat. The mistress fell to grieving and weeping over her children, but a great anger came upon our brave ancestor and he vowed to make the English pay.

He gathered his men around him and was for joining his friends who were fighting the English in a different part of Munster.

" 'It's only me wife and children I'm worried about,' he said. 'Who'll stay behind and take care of them?'

"There was an old bard in his household, a man of great wisdom and learning, famous for his poetry and wit. His name was Gorrane McEgan, and it was he who stepped forward and said: 'The years weigh upon me and it's not my feeble arm that will conquer the Sassenach. But I will take care of your lady and her babes if you will trust me with them.'

"The great O'Sullivan thanked the old bard warmly and took leave of his wife, who clung to him in the way of a woman, crying that it must be a heart of stone he had, to be deserting her. Then he went off with his men to uphold the honor of Ireland. Poor Gorrane was left behind with his weeping mistress and children, and he thought at first that the load of the world was on him, for not a bite nor a sup did he have to give them. And all around the enemy lurked, ready to pounce on them if they moved out of the shelter of the woods. First they must have a home and a place where they could lie down to sleep without fear. So Gorrane used his knowledge of secret places and took the fugitives to a cave in the mountains, so well covered with greenery that ye couldn't find it if ye were a nail's breadth away from it. It was a roomy cave, and he lit a charcoal fire and made beds of fern to lie on. Then he took his gun and went out to look for food. Alas! Too many had been shooting rabbits and squirrels and ne'er a one did he see. He was just going back sadly when he passed a steep rock, and looking up he saw an eagles' nest on an outjutting crag. A big parent bird came swooping down with a fat rabbit in its claws and the next minute the young eagles had fallen on it with loud screeches and were tearing it to bits, the way ye could see the fur fly. Gorrane put his finger to his nose and his eyes lit up. 'It's a breakfast I'm seeing, a fine savory breakfast!' he said, and hastened back to the cave. He consoled his mistress for his coming empty handed. 'Wait now till the morning and then I'll bring ye food as fine as ever ye've tasted,' he said.

"The rest of the day and part of the night he spent twisting a big strong rope of bogfir, and at the crack of dawn he wakened his son Patrick, a boy of fifteen years, and told him to come along. The astonished boy followed his father through the gloaming until they reached a mountain top whence they could look down on the eagles' nest. They were just in time to see one of the parent eagles soar off in search of food, leaving six screeching babies. 'Now, son,' said Gorrane. 'It's down into that nest

19

I'm wanting ye to go, and you're to tie the bills of those little monsters with bits of string so they can't eat.' 'But, Father darling,' said Pat, wondering greatly. 'If it's the birds ye want why can't we kill them and have done with them? There's little enough meat on them anyway. If that's the treat ye're after promising the mistress she must be in a bad way altogether!' 'Hold your prate, laddie,' said his father impatiently. 'There's no time to be telling ye the this and that of it. Do as I bid ye and tie the beaks of these creatures so they can't open them at all, then jerk the rope and I'll haul ye up again.'

"So it was done. Gorrane fastened the rope around his son's waist and lowered him carefully into the nest, frightening the little birds out of their wits. Pat then took hold of each fluttering eaglet and tied its bill firmly, after which he was safely drawn up. For an hour or so he and his father watched and waited. At last the parent birds returned, one with a rabbit and one with a grouse in its talons. They dropped their prey into the nest and flew off again. The poor little birds fell upon the feast but pecked vainly, for, sure enough, not the smallest piece could they bite off. Now Pat was let down again and grabbed the rabbit and the grouse, after which he freed the baby eagles' bills. Safely up again, he handed his prey to Gorrane, who cut off the precious meat and threw the skin and bones to the hungry birds, for wasn't it right that they should have something? Oh, the joy that was on the mistress and her children when they saw Gorrane and Pat return laden with food, and the gorgeous feast they made of it! But it's hard work the old eagles had from that day on, for they were obliged to feed a human family as well as their own. They must have wondered at the appetites of their youngsters.

"At last the Sassenach grew weary of the siege and left the neighborhood. Then O'Sullivan's wife and children could move to a place of greater plenty and comfort whilst the eaglets grew up and flew away. In this manner it was that our ancestors were saved and the mountain on which the birds nested is called to this day 'Nead an Iolair,' or 'Eagles' Nest.' "

When Father had finished, the children drew a deep breath for, though it was an old story, they were always thrilled to hear it.

"Were poets cleverer than other people in those days?" asked Michael.

"They were, son. They were the scholars, since the times of the old high kings, before even Saint Patrick came over. The chief poet came next to the king in rank, he was honored greatly and wore a mantle made of the finest bird feathers."

"Did Gorrane wear a mantle like that?"

21

"Ah, no. He lived much later, when the English were persecuting the bards because they kept the love of Ireland warm in the hearts of her people. When Queen Elizabeth came to rule our country she forbade the teaching of poetry, but the Irish bards couldn't be silenced. They gathered in hedges and ditches with their children and went on teaching history and Latin and the right use of the Gaelic, at the risk of their lives. It was rags they wore in those days."

"Like Paddy the Piper. Is he a bard, Father?" asked Brigid. Paddy the Piper, a traveling musician and the son of Mrs. O'Flaherty, who lived next door, was a great friend of the children.

Father smiled into the fire. "Maybe so," he said.

"Did Gorrane's son become a poet too?" asked Brigid again.

"Very likely," Father agreed.

"I would be proud to have been that boy, Father. He was brave, wasn't he?" said Michael.

"Pooh!" grumbled Francie. "Is it him ye call brave an' his father holding him by a rope all the time? It's loose I would have gone into that nest!"

"You would not," said Liam. "Mother wouldn't have let ye!"

They all laughed, but Mother said it was bedtime and

carried Francie into the other room, to his great disgust. Liam followed meekly. Though much stronger than his brother, his spirit was gentle. Francie, the delicate one, had the heart of a lion. Brigid and Michael sat up a little longer, chatting with their father. Then it was their turn, and, when they had said their prayers and were tucked under, Mother kissed them and drew the curtains. Outside the rain still fell in long silver streaks; the children heard its pitter-patter on the roof and fell asleep.

TWO

The Little Dog

THE next morning the sun peeped through the windows. The clouds had blown away during the night, and the wet world sparkled in the golden rays. The children were up and about as soon as they woke, delighted that the long spell of rain had passed while there were still a few days of their summer holidays left.

"Micky," cried Mother from the kitchen, where she was preparing breakfast, "will you fetch me some water?"

"I will, Mother," said Michael, stepping into his breeches.

The twins went with him. They liked to go to the well, but Mother would never allow them to go alone for fear they might fall in. Michael carried a bucket in each hand, and they trudged up the little road that led to the well. A sweet wind from the mountains carried the smell of heather in bloom, and the children breathed deeply. They had to pass Mrs. O'Flaherty's cottage; and Mrs. O'Flaherty, a lonely widow, kept a cow of uncertain temper. The twins were desperately afraid of the beast and stayed close to Michael. There was not a word out of them; they walked on tiptoes, gazing anxiously at Mrs. O'Flaherty's stable door. Indeed, the next minute the cow came charging through it, a wicked gleam in her eyes. The twins stood ready to run, but Michael was not frightened by a mere cow.

"Go on out of that!" he cried fiercely, putting down the buckets and waving his arms.

The cow looked surprised. Her head sank to one side, and she wondered whether the fun was worth the risk of attacking this bold boy.

"Will you get a move on, you contrary creature!"

shouted Michael, and the cow bethought herself, turned tail, and trotted into the meadow, to the great relief of Francie and Liam. But Mrs. O'Flaherty had heard the noise and planted herself in the doorway, shaking her fist at the boys.

"Is it me darling cow you're pestering again?" she cried angrily. "Will ye never leave the beast in peace, ye great strapping good-for-nothing! It's a wonder your mother doesn't tell ye to mind your own business for a change. . . ."

"If you'll teach your cow to do the same. . . ." Michael cried.

"Sure and she won't harm a fly if ye leave her alone," said Mrs. O'Flaherty. "Come here, Clementine darling."

The big cow went to her and was scratched between the horns, looking very meek and modest.

"There now, what am I telling ye, the beast is as quiet as a newborn lamb. Away with ye, and don't let me catch ye teasing her again." Mrs. O'Flaherty disappeared into the cottage, slamming the lower half of her door shut.

"God forgive her," said Michael, taking up the buckets again.

"I think Mrs. O'Flaherty is the spit and image of her own cow," cried Liam, who was tripping on gaily now the danger was past and had swiftly regained the use of his tongue.

"Or else the cow is the image of Mrs. O'Flaherty," added Francie.

Michael laughed. "She is a queer woman but she can't help it," he said. "She's cross because she is lonesome. Paddy the Piper is all she has in the world, and he's out on the road most of the time. Sure I wouldn't like to be her for a bag of gold."

"I wouldn't either," said Liam. "Not for wagons an' wagons full of gold! Would you, Francie?"

Francie's head went to one side. "You never know now," he muttered, thinking it over. "I might."

They had reached the well, which was a natural one, springing up from a cavity in the rocks. The water gleamed like crystal and long green ferns hung their tendrils into it. Michael filled his buckets, and the children returned without further trouble. When they passed Mrs. O'Flaherty's cottage, there was neither cow nor mistress to be seen.

Father was sitting up with his leg on a stool again; his ankle still smarted. He was glad the children had offered to take the donkey, for he would not have been able to go himself.

Brigid stood at the table slicing some bread to eat on the way, and Mother ladled out the stirabout. The boys, hungry from their exercise, fell to with a will.

"Did the cow come out?" Brigid asked, trying to butter bread with one hand and eat her stirabout with the other.

"Indeed she did!" cried Francie. "But she found her match, she did!"

"Meaning that you knocked her down yourself?" inquired Father, who was sitting by the fire with the stirabout on his knees.

Francie hung his head and blushed, but Liam spoke up in his defense. "Sure, he would have if he'd got the chance; but as soon as the creature set eyes on him, she ran as fast as if she had ten legs on her, she did."

Francie gave his brother a grateful look, and Liam didn't mind the others laughing—he was used to that.

It was time for Michael and Brigid to go. They put on their shoes—it was too far a journey to go barefooted—and their coats. Father called Michael to his side and said: "Mind now, boy, the money is needed, so be careful. There are many things can happen on the road. Don't let yourself be distracted, but keep your mind on your business and ye'll be all right."

"I will, Father," said Michael solemnly.

They still had to catch the donkey, and that was no small job, for the creature was half wild. This time they were in luck. They saw him in the fields close to the house, but as soon as they drew near, he galloped off, kicking his heels in the air. They had to chase him over a hill, across a little stream, and through tangled masses of brambles and gorse until they had him cornered. Michael held the donkey whilst Brigid tied the rope around his neck. He was a handsome animal, with long hair and soft furry ears. His large eyes looked sadly at his captors, but they showed him no mercy and he was led home triumphantly.

Mother stood in the door and handed them the bag of food and a blue saucepan. "I put in some praties with the bread," she said. "Ye'll be hungry, I'll warrant."

The children kissed their parents as though they were going away for weeks, then climbed on the donkey's back. It was a little crowded, but no matter.

"Well, God bless ye and safe home!" cried Mother as they started.

There was a little trouble when Mr. Murphy's geese came running onto the road, stretching their necks and trying to bite the donkey's legs. The donkey didn't like it and gave a jump which nearly threw off his riders. Michael cried out fiercely: "Arra! be gone with you!" and waved his arms at the geese, who gave up and waddled off in dignified silence. Soon they were on the main road to Kenmare, leaving their village behind them. The road mounted into the woods where trees spread huge branches over their heads, and the sun shone through the leaves throwing patterns on the white road. Birds twittered, ivy and moss clung to the gnarled tree trunks, and the sides of the road were green with maidenhair, Saint Patrick's cabbage, and clover. The donkey started to eat some and, finding it very appetizing, he settled down to a good feed and would not move, though the children shouted at him and thumped his thick hide. Michael got off and tugged at the rope, but even that did not help; the donkey was too well pleased where he was. So Michael pulled at one end of the rope and the

donkey at the other. The odds were even until Brigid
leaned back and pinched the donkey's tail. It gave the
creature such a turn, he ran right into the middle of the
road and started to gallop. Michael lost hold of the cord,
and Brigid, clinging to the donkey's neck as they raced
along, called out to him to catch it. It was easier said
than done; wild donkeys are good runners, and Michael
was out of practice. At least, that was what he said later
to justify himself. Poor Brigid could not control the
beast and as he hated the feel of the hard road on his
tender hoofs, he lurched aside and gave her a wild ride

31

through thickets and bogs and down such steep hills that if she had not turned around the other way and caught hold of his tail, instead of his neck, it would have gone ill with her.

Poor Michael was running breathless after them; he had to keep them in sight or he'd lose them entirely. Less nimble at crossing thickets than the donkey, he became a sorry spectacle, covered with scratches and bruises. But Brigid's wits had been busy, and though it took most of her strength to keep from falling, she managed to catch hold of the rope and twist a loop in it at the far end. This she threw over a stout stump as they passed it and the donkey was caught.

There was a long pause. Then Brigid wearily tumbled off the animal, trembling with weakness after her dizzy ride. Michael arrived in as bad a condition as could be. Only the donkey felt quite calm; it was all in the day's work for him.

"I'm glad we're selling the beast," said Michael, glaring at him. Brigid said:

"Well, he is a donkey, isn't he? You can't expect a donkey to act like a horse!"

They sat down to rest awhile, and Michael tried to patch his clothes together again. There was a big tear in his coat which Brigid mended with a safety pin.

"You don't look too bad," she consoled him.

The worst was that they had no idea how to get back to the road. Michael climbed a tree to find the way. He said he saw some smoke and that there was sure to be a road where there was a chimney; so they went in that direction. As they approached the spot they discovered that the smoke rose not from the chimney of a house, but from the open fire of a gypsies' camp.

Several swarthy men were playing cards near the fire on which a pot of soup was simmering. At least it smelled like soup. On the steps of an old caravan under the trees a few dirty children were playing and a woman was hanging up some gray-looking wash. Michael thought it better to avoid the camp because the men looked so rough, and luckily he saw the road not far off. They had nearly reached it when the whimpering and crying of a dog in pain made them stop. They looked around and saw one of the big men beating a poor little half-starved mongrel with his large hobnailed boot.

Michael could never bear to see an animal mistreated, so he ran back and shouted: "Stop that this minute!"

Several of the men looked round in astonishment and the big man who had been beating the dog stopped and advanced towards Michael, holding the dog by the scruff of his neck. Michael felt his heart tremble when he looked up at this huge fellow. He was so solid looking, with big hands and angry eyes and a terrible, dark beard. Michael would have run like a hare if he had not remembered that an Irishman never turns his back to the enemy.

"What was that you said?" the man grumbled in a threatening voice, rolling his eyes.

Michael dared not look at him, but he spoke up bravely: "Ye shouldn't be beating a poor wee dog like that."

"An' who'll tell me what I should do or what I shouldn't?" said the man, and the men around the fire sniggered. The woman called out in a high voice: "Arra, Charlie, leave the brat alone for God's sake, will ye! Ye've got us into trouble enough these last days!"

The man had made a movement as if he wanted to try his boot on Michael next, but the woman's words seemed to have an effect, for, instead, he laughed scornfully and gave the dog a kick that sent it flying into the bushes.

"If ye're so sorry for the brute, ye can take it an' welcome," he shouted. "It's brought me nothing but bad luck, an' may it bring ye more, me fairy prince!"

"Sure, and I'll take it, if it's this way ye're treating it all the time!" cried Michael indignantly. But the man had gone back to the camp and paid no more heed to him.

The little dog had fallen among some prickly brambles and was whimpering softly. Michael's heart ached with pity when he ran to Brigid, who waited for him on the road. Her courage had deserted her the moment she saw the blackbearded man.

"He says we can have the dog!" Michael told her. "Shall we take him with us?"

"Good for you!" cried Brigid. "Of course we'll take him, the poor helpless creature. Wait, I'll get out a piece of bread." She rummaged in the food bag.

The little dog was quite hurt and lay licking his sore legs, whimpering fitfully. Brigid crept close to him and coaxed him with the bread in her hand. Poor little fellow, he was probably starved; it was little trouble to make him come, though he trembled with fear and held his tail between his shivering legs. The children grabbed him up joyously and ran to their tethered donkey. They were on it in a twinkling, Michael urging it into a fast trot, for fear the gypsies might change their minds. They were well out of reach of the gypsies before the donkey stopped running, and then the road became so steep that the children dismounted. Brigid had hardly looked at the dog yet, she had been so anxious to get away. Now she lavished sympathy on him, and he responded by licking her hands and face.

"We must keep him, Michael. Do you think they'll let us?" she asked anxiously.

Michael shrugged his shoulders. "Maybe they will, and maybe they won't," he said.

"Oh, they must!" cried Brigid. "They can't let the poor beast starve, when it has suffered so much already." She kissed its wet little nose. "Sure, and he may be useful too; he'll be a good watch dog, won't you, doggie? What'll we call him, Michael?"

"Let's call him Bran," Michael suggested, "after Finn's magic dog the teacher told us about. Maybe this one is magic too, maybe he is an enchanted prince, and he will help us because we delivered him."

"Do you believe such things *really* happen?" Brigid asked. The idea frightened her.

"I do, and I don't," said Michael. "Sometimes I don't believe there's anything at all except what you can touch or see, and then again I think the world is full of fairies. Sometimes of an evening when the mist comes creeping low over the fields and the moon hangs round and red in the skies, I think I can see the little people sitting in a fairy ring."

They had long left the woods behind, and now the mountain winds ruffled their hair. Down below, the glen smiled in green and gold, jeweled with glittering lakes. They could see the white houses of their village peeping through the dark green of the woods and beyond, the blue bay shimmered and shone. At this height the mountains were bare; sheep cropped the stiff grass and ran away with funny little jerks, tinkling their bells at the approach of the children. Blue peaks lifted their heads one behind the other, now dipped in shade, now gilt with sunshine, losing themselves in the haze of distance.

"There is the Eagles' Nest," said Michael, pointing to a ragged mountain top in front of them. "I wonder where that cave of Gorrane's is. It can't have disappeared, but you never hear anyone talk about it. We ought to be looking for it some day!"

"Maybe we will find it, and then we'll have a grand hiding place in case the English come back on us again!" cried Brigid.

A few minutes later the children reached the famous tunnel which had been bored through the mountainside to save traffic the tortuous climb over the top. After some hesitation the donkey was persuaded to enter the dark passage and there was a general feeling of relief when they emerged safely at the other end. At this point the road dropped again, and they could see it winding down into the valley of the Sheen. They breathed deeply, now that they had the mountain ridge behind them. They felt more secure from the gypsies, who might want their dog back again. Once Brigid jumped with fright when a horn tooted close behind her, and she had just enough time to drag the donkey out of the way of a whirring automobile as it dashed past, leaving a stink behind.

"Bah!" said Michael, holding his nose. "That's the worst of main roads, there is no getting away from the cars."

"I like the old roads," Brigid murmured dreamily. "Those with grass and flowers sprouting between the stones. They are friendly and keep ye company as ye go—look now, how this road seems to be running away from us as fast as it can. It hasn't got a word to say for itself!"

Michael laughed. "Sure enough, that's true," he said.

The donkey must have spent all his wild spirits, for he behaved beautifully the rest of the way, though he sniffed at the lovely bits of pasture here and there, feeling very sorry for himself. It was easier going down. The sun was getting hot, and they were glad when they reached the welcome shelter of trees again.

"Can you tell us, ma'am, where Farmer Flynn lives?" Michael asked politely of a woman who came up the road.

"Farmer Flynn?" said the woman, stopping and wrinkling her forehead. "Let me see . . . it might be on this side of the bay, and then again, it might be on t'other. . . ."

"Thank ye kindly, ma'am," said Michael gravely. "That's very helpful."

"It's a pleasure," said the woman and hobbled off, leaving Michael and Brigid staring after her.

"We'll have to ask someone else," Michael said, and he hailed a boy on a bicycle. "Can you tell us where Farmer Flynn lives?"

"Surely I can; don't I bring him the bread every day? On t'other side of the bay he lives, down the Kilgarvan road, second turn to your right, fifth house to the left, an' ye have it in your hand!"

That was clear enough. The children were soon crossing the lovely new bridge over the Kenmare estuary, and walking down the Kilgarvan road. Farmer Flynn's was a nice little whitewashed house. Chickens ran clucking out of the way as the children walked up the flagged path to the door. A woman came out to see what was the matter.

"Well, if it isn't the donkey!" she exclaimed. "Come in, children. Did ye walk all the way? Well now, aren't ye great! Ye'll have to sit down and drink a glass of milk. My, but it's a darling donkey!" She clasped her hands, gazing at the animal with admiration. Michael forgot his previous anger with the beast and swelled with pride, but Brigid was overwhelmed with pity for it, for the poor dumb creature did not know it was about to be sold. She put down Bran and flung both arms round the donkey's neck, kissing its warm hide.

41

"There now, bless your heart," said the woman. "Ye need not take on so. We'll be good to him, won't we, Neddie?" She held out some grass to the donkey, who snapped it up eagerly with velvet lips, looking out of the corner of his large brown eyes for more. "And you've got a dog too, I see," said Mrs. Flynn, bending down to stroke Bran. "But dear me! It's very thin. Are ye sure you're giving it enough to eat? Dogs need good care, ye know." She looked reproachfully at the children, who hastened to explain that it was none of their doing. They told how they happened to get the dog.

Mrs. Flynn pitied the animal greatly and praised the children for rescuing it from those bad gypsies.

"I'll take the creature meself if ye'll let me," she said. "I don't have a dog, and this looks a nice little body to me."

The children would not hear of it.

"Oh, please, ma'am," said Brigid. "Isn't the donkey enough for ye? We do so want to keep Bran, if Father and Mother will let us!"

Mrs. Flynn smilingly assured her that she would not dream of taking their treasure away. "But if he is too troublesome at home, ye know where ye can bring him," she added.

"What's all this?" It was a man's voice, and a farmer

stepped from behind the house to look at them with a pair of the bluest eyes the children had ever seen. "So ye've brought the donkey," he said. "And a handsome one it is. Tell me, is he as good as he looks?"

"He runs very fast," said Michael truthfully. "And he doesn't need much care. He knows his own mind."

"Ye don't mean that he is obstinate?" said the farmer, raising his eyebrows.

"No, sir," said Michael hastily. "It's just that betimes he might be mistaking what you say for the opposite, God help him."

"Well, I think he is a darling donkey," said Mrs. Flynn, who had quite fallen in love with his soft looks. "Come along in now, and I'll give ye some milk before ye go, and that poor starved doggie must have something too." She took them into a lovely kitchen and poured out two glasses of foaming milk and put some cold potatoes and meat on a saucer for Bran.

The children were thirsty and drank as fast as manners permitted, but it was nothing compared to the swiftness with which the dog bolted down his food. He actually began to fill out before their eyes. The farmer handed Michael the money for the donkey in an envelope and told him to be careful of it. Michael had to put his name on a receipt, which meant that if he lost the money the farmer would not pay it over again. When that was settled, Mr. Flynn asked his wife for a glass of milk to keep the children company.

"Ye're never satisfied, Shamus," his wife remarked. "I do believe ye'd eat the hind leg off a donkey!"

"Not off our donkey!" cried Brigid alarmed, but her brother nudged her. "Don't be foolish, she's only joking."

"What's that hole in the wall there?" asked Brigid presently, pointing to a little round hole beside the window.

"That's a bullet hole," said the farmer proudly. "I keep it in memory of the 'troubles.' There was fierce shooting around these parts."

"Shooting, was there?" cried Michael with sparkling eyes. He well knew that the "troubles" meant the last war with England.

"Me mother tells us of the bad times they were, and how me father was on the run and she home alone with Biddy and me. . . ."

"Bad times, indeed," the farmer said. "But there were some grand moments when we put the enemy to flight, and we did get nearly all we wanted. That's the main thing."

44

"Please tell us something about the troubles. Did you have the Black-and-Tans here?" asked Michael.

"Didn't we, then! Wasn't the whole country swarming with them and they dressed in black and brown like real bloodhounds and acting like them too? That's how they got their name. No Irishman was allowed to be armed when the English ruled the country, and you could not carry so much as a pistol without risking your life. The English bloodhounds would search us in shops, on the street, in cars, any old place. I mind one day when I was carrying a heavy gun meself and got into a tram. The Black-and-Tans stopped it, and I would have been kilt entirely if they had found me gun. But a young woman sat next to me wrapped in her black cloak. When the soldiers stepped inside, she took the gun from me and hid it under her cloak. They didn't search women in those days and so we both escaped, thanks to the pluck of that girl!"

"Ooh!" said Brigid. "I would never have dared. . . ."

"Did ye ever see the girl again?" asked Michael.

The farmer smiled, and looked at his wife, who blushed. "I married her," said he.

Brigid looked at plump Mrs. Flynn with new eyes.

"This farm belonged to me father then," the farmer continued. "Do ye see those bushes at the back of the garden? One day word was sent to me father that the Black-and-Tans were on their way to raid us, so we hurriedly hid all our guns in the bushes and went to sleep peacefully, thinking we would be safe if the enemy came. No one disturbed us that night. It had been a false alarm, and well it was, for the next morning when we looked into the garden, the sight we saw was enough to turn a frog pink. Our precious guns, that we had hidden so carefully, were hanging on bare branches like toys on a Christmas tree for any fool to see."

"What had happened?" asked Michael laughing at the farmer's droll face.

"The goats had got loose and they were mightily fond of foliage. So they nibbled all the leaves off the bushes, leaving them as bare as a flagpole and just as notorious. Sure we'd have been lost entirely if God hadn't had mercy on us."

"Oh!" cried Michael. "I wish those things would happen now."

"Whisht, child, ye don't know what ye're saying," said the farmer's wife. "Sure, Shamus, ye shouldn't be filling their heads with foolishness, making them think it's grand to be fighting. It's time for you to be going back now," she added. "It's a long way, and ye won't have a donkey to ride on."

46

"Yes, Michael, we must be going," cried Brigid. They thanked the farmer and his wife very much for their kindness and coaxed Bran away from the fire, where he had fallen asleep.

"Well, goodby, children, and safe home!"

"Goodby, and thank ye!"

THREE

The Lonely Road

"LET'S have something to eat before we go back," Michael suggested, when they were out on the road again, the sun warm on their heads. "That milk has made me hungry." He jumped over a gate into a field.

"I see some fine big stones here for our oven!"

Brigid went running along after him, Bran at her heels, and the two children soon gathered enough stones to build an oven, with the open side facing the breeze. Then they looked for dry sticks and straw, which they piled in a heap. Brigid took the pan to the nearest cottage to ask for water. When she came back, walking carefully so as not to spill a drop, a puff of smoke told her that Michael had already started the fire. Brigid put down her pan to help him. He had lit some straw and now he fed the sudden flame with little sticks and pieces of dry bark. The ground was still wet with yesterday's rain and the sticks sizzled when Michael stuck them into the fire.

Brigid gathered more fuel and Bran helped her, carrying twigs in his mouth and laying them at Michael's feet.

"There! Isn't he the bright dog!" cried his new master proudly.

They soon had the fire going nicely, so they put on the pan with water into which they had dropped the potatoes, then sat down in the grass, waiting for them to cook. Bran stretched himself lazily at their feet, and all around insects hummed and flowers and grass waved in the breeze. The children lay down, enjoying the sun on their bare legs and arms, breathing deeply the hay-scented air.

Now and again the fire burned low and had to be fed

with more sticks. Then all was quiet, and a delicious drowsiness stole over the children. Brigid actually dropped asleep for a moment, waking with a start when the water boiled over into the fire with a hiss.

"This is grand," said Michael, who lay on his back with his eyes shut. "We'll be well rested for the journey home."

"I don't like going back," grumbled Biddy. She poked the potatoes with a stick to see if they were nearly done, but no, they were as hard as pebbles. "I'm afraid of them gypsies."

"Small blame to you. I'm in dread of them meself," Michael admitted. "They put little enough value on their dog when they had him, but they're sure to be sorry they gave him to us, and they're murthersome creatures!"

"Oh, Micky!" pleaded Brigid, round-eyed with horror. "*Please* don't go back that way again. Is there no other road at all we could take?"

"Indeed there is," cried Michael, sitting bolt upright. "I'd forgotten. There is a road past Kilgarvan which goes right over the mountains instead of through a tunnel like the other."

Brigid could not help thinking of the money Michael carried. "Is it not too far, and are there not robbers along that road?" she asked cautiously.

Michael scratched his ear. "Why would there be robbers," he asked, "when it's only farmers live there and they not rich? Wouldn't it be more likely the robbers would keep to the roads that are traveled by the rich folk in their cars? No, now I come to think of it, it would be safer to go the long way with all the money on me."

"Oh, I'm glad," said Brigid, most willing to be convinced.

They now turned their attention to the dinner for the praties were nice and soft. They fished them out of the pan and put them on the grass to cool. Michael opened the bag and took out the bread and some salt. Bran was all eyes and nose and sat up on his hind legs to show he was ready to eat. Michael threw him some bread and Bran fell to, wagging his tail so fast that Brigid was afraid it would come off. The potatoes tasted scrumptious. They were never so tasty when eaten in the kitchen out of the big black pot.

When they had finished their meal, the children gathered up the papers and peels and burned them, after which they stamped out the fire, making sure no spark remained. They also cleaned the pan on the grass for it was black with smoke. Then they set off on their long tramp home.

At Kilgarvan Michael asked a woman, who was leaning on the half-door of her cottage, the way to Glengarriff. The woman looked at them in astonishment.

51

"Surely, ye're not going that far, the three of you?" she said, with a doubtful glance at the skinny little dog.

"We've come from there this morning," Michael explained proudly.

"Is it all the way from Glengarriff ye've come?" cried the woman, throwing up her hands. "Faith, but you must have powerful legs!"

Michael felt a little foolish and when the woman had pointed out the right road he started off, but Brigid hung back and whispered: "Do ye think there'd be robbers on the way?"

The woman laughed heartily. "Robbers, is it? And what would they be robbing then? Is it sixpence they'd be wanting to risk their necks for? Surely the likes of you won't tempt them!"

Brigid would have told her of the money they carried but Michael dragged her off.

"Thank you kindly, ma'am," he said, touching his forelock. "We'd better be going now. It's getting late."

"Goodby, and may God and Saint Patrick bless you," cried the woman. She looked after them, still laughing as they took the mysterious road into the mountains, the little rescued dog close at their heels.

It was indeed a lonely road. They could follow its

curves for miles and miles until it lost itself in a blue haze, and it seemed to beckon them on, saying:

> "Follow ye me, follow ye me,
> I hold treasures new and old;
> Fields I know which gleam like gold,
> Over the hills and down by the sea.
>
> "Follow ye me, follow ye me,
> I know places weird and eerie;
> None who follow me grow weary,
> So you will see, so you will see!
>
> "Follow ye me, follow ye me,
> I can show you ancient bridges,
> High and mighty mountain ridges,
> If you'll agree, if you'll agree. . . ."

They were in luck, for a man in a cart overtook them and asked if they would like a lift. The children gladly assented, and they climbed onto his rough, springless, straw-covered cart. The big, bony, sleepy horse jogged up the hill and they rattled along for several miles until the man stopped at a farmhouse and told them they would have to get off.

They thanked him fervently, for it was a long weary walk the ride had spared them. As they looked back, they could see the road winding down to Kilgarvan, where the cottages lay snuggled against the green. Sheaves of wheat gleamed golden in the late sunlight, casting their lengthening shadows on the ground; the distant mountains lifted their purple peaks against the sky. But the road before them seemed endless yet, and with a sigh they trudged on, Bran frisking around them. The little bit of food he'd eaten seemed to have done the dog a lot of good. Already he showed high spirits and accepted the children as his new masters.

They soon left the friendly valley far behind and wandered amidst weirdly shaped rocks which loomed darker and darker in the waning light. It was so still up there. Not even the bleat of a sheep disturbed the silence.

"Isn't it lonesome?" whispered Brigid. "Paddy the Piper says there are bad 'pookas' in the mountains who lie in wait for weary travelers." She shivered.

"It makes me feel queer meself," Michael admitted, looking around him. Sometimes they were wrapped in the shade of the rocks. It was easy to imagine the dark mountains filled with goblins, but Brigid said bravely: "I don't mind. No evil can touch us if we but say a 'Hail Mary.' "

The children held each other's hands, repeating the prayer; the dog looking on with proper gravity.

After that, they felt better and took new courage, which

they needed, for the road was long and steep, and they felt weary. They had hopes that once they reached the top of the hill the worst would be over, but there was another hill after that and again another. They were mounting higher and higher, the very air seemed to grow colder, and the sun dropped lower and lower, gilding the fringes of the sky. When they had climbed the highest and steepest hill of all, they held onto each other in amazement. There was nothing beneath them but a sheer precipice and far below they could see a valley that was unknown to them, with a river running through the middle of it.

The children sat down weakly on a stone, their breath taken away by the suddenness and grandeur of the scenery. In truth, they might be on the top of the world, the way they could see for miles and miles in front of them. To the right and left the mountains lifted their heads proudly in the late orange light of the setting sun.

"Heaven help us," said Michael, watching the road wind itself down into the valley. "If it's all that way we still have to go, how will we ever get home at all?"

The children were silent for a moment, thinking of their mother's anxiety and the trust that had been placed in them; but Brigid was not one to keep on regretting what could not be helped.

"It serves us right for our foolishness," she said. "We

should have known better than to go a road we'd never gone before. What's done can't be undone, so we'd better be making up our minds that we'll be on the road all night and start looking for a place to sleep."

"You're a sensible woman," said Michael. "We'll do so."

The children soon found that the downward course was narrow and perilous. To their left the rocky wall rose steeply; to the right the precipice yawned. Besides, the road was old and had crumbled off in places. It took all their attention to keep from falling.

"It's great good luck we don't have to walk this road in the dark, Biddy," said Michael "Mind yourself, walk easy— that stone is loose there. This is a wicked road!"

They shuffled along, holding onto the rocky wall, until the road widened again as it sloped and curved into the valley. They had just left the bad parts behind them when the sun set and the orange sky paled behind the purple mountains. Stars began to twinkle overhead and the chill of the approaching night made the children shiver in their coats.

"Wherever will we find a place to sleep?" muttered Michael. "I hope it won't rain!"

"We'll ask at some farm whether we may sleep in the haystack," said Brigid.

As the road dropped lower, they could hear the river

rushing between the meadows. They saw lighted cottage windows, twinkling here and there in the twilight. It had grown quite dark when they reached the first farmhouse. A dog barked when they went up to it.

"Who's there?" cried a voice, and a man stood in the doorway, dark against the light.

"Please, sir, we're only two lost children and we want to make a bed in your haystack if you'll let us, sir," said Michael politely, holding onto Bran for fear of the big dog, which hurled itself forward barking fiercely, but which was restrained by its owner.

"It's no lost children ye are at all!" cried the farmer angrily. "I can see by that cur in your arms that it's from the gypsies ye are. Well I know that dog! Didn't I chase it out of me turnip patch the day before yesterday, and it digging holes all over the place? Arra, be off with ye! I won't have any gypsies in me hay!"

The farmer slammed his door shut, and the children went back sadly to the road.

"The gypsies have been here then," Michael whispered, peering anxiously at the dark hedges bordering the road. "I hope they're not here now."

"Are ye going to try another farmhouse, Michael?"

"I'm afraid to. They might think we were gypsies again, or maybe they'd lock up Bran for a stray dog."

59

"Where will we sleep then?" Brigid nearly cried, for she was very, very tired.

"I'm looking for some field or a lone stack of hay." And Michael strained his eyes trying to see through the darkness.

The roaring of the river waxed stronger and stronger as they went on. There were trees to the right and left of them and the wind whispered in the leaves making queer and creepy sounds that startled the children and made them feel they were secretly pursued by the gypsies. Michael carried the dog in his arms for fear it would get lost.

It was hard to find a place to lie down, but at last they thought they saw a meadow. Michael first climbed the low fence and Brigid followed, clumsy from weariness. They scrambled through some thornbushes and entered the field. Though they could see little, they felt the ground soft and sloppy under their feet.

"I don't believe this is a good place, Micky," said Brigid in a tired little voice. "We won't be able to lie down here. It's too damp."

"Maybe it'll be better further on," Michael suggested.

They plodded on for a way, mud clinging to their shoes. At last they lay down on what they thought was a nice, soft patch of grass. It was good to be off their feet, and they felt so drowsy they could have slept at once. But

Bran fidgeted and barked. When they let him loose, he pulled at Brigid's skirt.

"Whatever can he be wanting?" the girl asked, sitting upright and opening her eyes. She gave a startled little cry. "Look, Micky! Will-o'-the-wisps!" For the dark ground around her was covered with little moving lights, like so many diamonds. Michael sat up too.

"They're glowworms," he said. "I never saw so many before." The children gazed in fascination at the little green worms which lit up and darkened fitfully. Bran barked again and gave another tug at Brigid's skirt, and a sudden fear cleared the fog of sleepiness out of her head.

"Oh, Michael, I'm sinking. This is a bog!" she cried. "It's no field at all. We'll be drowned if we stay."

They had been too tired to notice how the ground that had seemed so firm had gradually softened, water oozing up in many places.

"It's the dog saved us," said Michael gratefully, when they were back on the road again. "He knew it was no place to lie down in. Faith, I was so tired I could have slept anywhere."

Brigid shivered. "It's the cold keeps meself awake," she said. "I'd be glad to sleep on the road, I'm that weary. But I put on a thin frock and me coat isn't warm enough."

"Take mine then," Michael offered generously, remov-

61

ing his coat. "And give me yours. Mine is thicker and you need it more. I have a flannel shirt as well."

"You're a darling!" Brigid cried. "It's fine and warm I am now."

They still hadn't found a place to sleep and their steps dragged on wearily. They passed another farm and saw a haystack beside it, or rather two of them, close together. There was no sound of dog or man, and the children crept forward until they reached the stacks. They tried to climb one, but had to give up for the stack was too high and too steep and slippery. So they pulled off some hay to make a bed on the ground between the two huge piles and laid themselves down with Bran between them. Brigid fell asleep at once from sheer exhaustion, but poor Michael was cold in his sister's thin coat and felt the ground very hard under the few handfuls of hay. Wisps of hay crept under his clothes and down his neck tickling him "something fierce," as he told Brigid, who was wakened by his scratching and fidgeting.

"Please let's go on," he said. "It's stiff and tired I am of lying in this place. Sure we'd be better off walking the road."

The short sleep had refreshed Brigid. She would have liked some more, but she felt cold again, and perhaps Michael was right. It would be healthier to keep moving.

They tottered onto their feet again and resumed their journey.

The black sky over their heads sparkled with millions of stars; the river sang a little song which they could somehow understand:

"When the brilliant sun is gone,
I keep rippling, rippling on,
Ever streaming, never weary,
Though the night be long and dreary.

"Through the stillness and the shadows,
Past the dusky, fragrant meadows,
Babbling on from bend to bend,
I flow forward to the end.

"Overhead a thousand eyes
Wink and twinkle from the skies,
And my waves reflect their light
Till I'm decked with jewels bright.

"Star-bespangled, like a king,
I speed onward and I sing
Of the mighty distant sea
That is calling, calling me."

"Hsst! Listen!" cried Brigid. "Did you hear a man's footsteps?" The children held their breath. There was no sound. "Ye don't think the gypsies are on our track now, do ye?" she asked. "They might have followed us."

"I don't hear anything," whispered Michael, listening intently.

"Maybe I was wrong then," said Brigid. "Oh, let's sit down a minute and rest ourselves. I'm so tired ye could knock me down with a feather."

They chose a low wall; it was damp with the heavy dew, but they were past minding such trifles. They gazed up at the stars and the small sickle of the moon.

"Can ye tell me whether it's waning or new?" asked Brigid.

"Ye can always know it by the letter it makes when you hold up a stick to it. If it's a *p*, it's coming *up*, and if it's a *d*, it's going *down*," said Michael, airing his wisdom.

"Then it's new!" cried Brigid. "We've seen it without glass, so we're allowed a wish." She shut her eyes tight.

"I wish we may keep Bran," she thought, "and that he may be a fairy prince and bring us luck!"

Michael's wish was more serious. "I wish I may bring the money safe home and that Father won't be mad at me for taking the long way back," he thought, feeling for his pocket.

Suddenly he grew alarmed searching for the familiar envelope and not finding it.

"Me money!" he cried, the sweat breaking out on him as he feared the worst. "It's gone!"

Brigid's eyes grew round with fear. "But ye can't have lost it," she said. "Ye've been so careful!"

Michael was in despair. "It must be by the haystacks I dropped it, or maybe in the bogs and then it's lost. . . . Oh! It's the fool I am. God forgive me!" He ran back up the road to see if he could still find it.

"Wait, Michael!" cried Brigid. "Maybe Bran will help us—dogs are good smellers."

"Faith, and that's true," said Michael with a sudden hope, and he tried to make Bran go, but, though the dog was willing to do anything and jumped up against his little master, licking his hands, he did not understand what was wanted.

"Think a minute," said Brigid, too tired to start on a wild goose chase. "Where *can* ye have lost it?"

The night wind ruffled their hair, owls hooted, and the leaves on the trees tittered like wicked elves. The children could hear tiny sounds like the fluttering of many wings and the tripping of many feet.

"Maybe the fairies got it," Brigid said awestruck.

"Or the gypsies," whispered Michael, who feared that wild men might be lurking behind the dark trees. "But the money is gone, and we have small chance of seeing it back." His voice broke into a sob.

Brigid could stand it no longer. She sat down in the

middle of the road and burst into tears. Michael soon followed her example, and Bran was so affected that he dropped on his haunches and howled.

There the three of them sat and cried, the stars twinkling down on them. Brigid's tears were flowing so fast that she groped in her pocket for a handkerchief, but instead she felt something thin and hard like paper and drew it out. It was the envelope with money!

"It's fools we are altogether!" she cried, laughing through her tears. "We're forgetting that ye gave me your coat to wear, and here the money is safe and sound!"

66

The children felt so happy they danced up and down on the road, Bran jumping around them with joyful barks.

"Oh! It's glad I am to have it back!" said Michael, hugging the envelope tight. "Now I'll put it in me breeches pocket, and there'll be no more mistakes, please God!"

It was no hardship to walk on now; happiness had dispelled their weariness. Though their feet were sore and swollen, they went ahead bravely, longing to be home and have the money safe.

Most of the short summer night was already spent. The darkness was ebbing from minute to minute leaving a cool gray mist. Birds stirred in the bushes, a cock crowed, and far away another answered. Presently the skyline blushed to herald the rising sun—a new day had dawned.

There was a promise of fine weather in the hazy blue of the sky, and the daylight gave the children new courage. Brigid longed for the sun for she was almost frozen with the cold.

As soon as it grew lighter, Michael felt ashamed of wearing a girl's coat and made Brigid give his back to him. Brigid shivered in her own thin one and impatiently watched the reddening sky. Michael's chief trouble was hunger. He wanted to run.

"What's keeping you?" he asked of Brigid when her

weary steps lagged. "Come, we'll have a song and it'll help you walk!"

He burst into the national anthem, and Brigid joined him, the two of them singing at the top of their voices and Bran barking the refrains. The noise echoed from the mountains and back again. Watch dogs began to howl furiously from farms near and far. All the creatures in the neighborhood down to the snails on the leaves woke up with a start. The valley, so still an hour before, now rang with tumultuous sound.

"How the farmers will love being wakened so early!" cried Michael, pausing a minute to take breath. "Serves them right for not letting us have one little haystack!"

"Look, there's Bantry Bay!" cried Brigid, welcoming her old friend gladly. There it lay, smooth and silvery, curving in and out of the rocky coast. As they watched, the sun burst forth in all its glory, chasing away the lingering shadows of the night and turning to gold the silver of the sea.

Brigid stretched out her numb hands to the first rays. Never before had she felt so fully the gladness of daybreak. But Michael urged her to hurry.

"I've a ravenous hunger on me, Biddy. I'll be eating you in a minute if ye don't make haste!"

68

"Och, Micky, it's easy for you to talk, but me feet are so painful I can hardly move."

"Well," said Michael, dragging her along impatiently, "I'm telling you it is serious. If I don't get a nice fat piece of bacon inside me soon, I'll do something wicked."

He fairly ran up the road which led home, his head filled with the thought of sausages, nice fat sausages, dripping with grease.

Father and Mother were far too relieved when they saw the truants stagger into the kitchen to scold them for the anxiety they had caused, though Mother had hardly slept all night. The twins were the first to discover Bran and to draw attention to him with delighted outcries, and Michael tried to explain and eat at the same time, whilst Brigid fell asleep over her stirabout.

Michael proudly handed the money to his father, who still had his foot on a stool, and Mother packed Brigid off to bed for the poor girl was too far spent even to eat. Michael felt so good after two plates of stirabout and six rashers of bacon that he was eager to tell what had happened, and Mother and Father and the twins were spellbound listening to so many adventures.

The twins were very sorry for Bran and begged that he might stay. But Father said it was an added expense, and

Mother feared the dog might be ill-mannered and wild, having been brought up by gypsies. The three boys pleaded so ardently, however, that neither Father nor Mother could find the heart to refuse them.

"He may stay if Michael looks after him and takes care that he is no bother and little expense," said Father, and Michael promised. So Bran became a member of the O'Sullivan household.

FOUR

Bold Bran

IT WAS quite a new experience for Bran to live in a house. He had been born in the gypsies' camp and had known nothing better all his life than the dust of the roads and the scramble through thickets and thorns, with a kick and a blow from one of the men whenever he tried to creep near the fire or secure himself a bite of food.

Now he had a fine little bed in the chimney corner, which Michael had made for him out of an old potato sack. Mother fed him regularly at mealtimes and he became sleek and round. Instead of being beaten he was often fondled so that he could hardly believe his luck.

There were many things he had to learn still, for not having been bred a house dog, he had very bad manners. Not only did he make a loud noise when eating, for all dogs do that, but he didn't know better than to snatch away the food from under Mother's hand when she was preparing it. Nor had he sense enough to see that Mother's hat was not meant to be eaten. The chickens also had a lot to suffer from him for he dearly loved a chase. Altogether he made so many mistakes that Mother began to be sorry she had let him stay, though he did look coaxingly at her now and then from out of his large brown eyes.

But when Mother once said: "Well, I'm thinking we'd better be sending the bold little creature to Farmer Flynn's after all," there arose such howls from the children that she had not the heart to repeat it, even when the neighbors came in again and again to complain of Bran's bad behavior.

The children had been frightened by Mother's words and they did all they could to shield Bran's misdeeds from her. One day, when he had taken Mother's knitting between his teeth and had run round the yard dragging the tangled wool through the mud, the twins were able to pull him away from it just before Mother ran out to see what was up. When she saw her knitting lying spoiled and torn in a puddle she nearly cried and said: "It's that rascal of a dog again, I'll warrant." But Francie cried out eagerly: "No, no, it was not him. I did it meself!" whilst Liam protested: "No, it was me!" The two of them were actually fighting for the honor of the deed until Mother lost patience and locked them up in the barn after boxing their ears soundly. Then Bran got a nice big bone from her to make up for having been unjustly accused.

Mrs. O'Flaherty hated the dog. The first day after his arrival, he had taken a fancy to Clementine and had chased her all over the field till Mrs. O'Flaherty shooed him away with her broom. She scolded Michael for it afterwards.

"Bad luck to ye. Is there no pity in ye at all, at all, to set that murthersome mongrel onto me sweet Clementine. She's sick after it, poor dear-she lost her wind entirely and small blame to her! Don't let me catch that dog near her again or I'll break all the bones in his body! So I will!"

After which Michael took care to keep Bran away though the dog had a fondness for the cow that would make him sneak back at odd times to bark at her until one of the children discovered him and dragged him off.

Altogether Mother was not a bit sorry when the school opened again. Francie and Liam were to go for the first time. They were only five and rather young, but Mother said she was anxious for some peace.

"It's all very fine for you, Mother. You don't have to be

sitting on hard benches and keeping your mouth shut all the time!" grumbled Michael, who was greatly out of humor on the morning of the first schoolday because he could not find his books. "Did you see them anywheres, Mother? Did you, Bridy? Where can they be? I've looked everywhere!"

But no one had seen them at all, so Michael gave up the hunt and sat on the doorstep with a sour face, throwing pebbles at the chickens.

When Mother had washed and dressed the twins, she went to look for Michael's books though Brigid told her it was a shame and he could do it himself. She was perfectly right, of course, but mothers will be mothers.

As soon as the watchful eyes had turned from the twins, those little vagabonds sneaked off, trying to snatch a little play before the iron hand of discipline would close upon them. They rushed to their favorite rock in front of the house, which had been polished bright by their breeches. Then, scrambling to the top, they slithered down swiftly, hitting the ground with a thud. Only this one glorious slide did they have before Michael noticed them and called:

"Mother! Will ye look at Francie and Liam spoiling their good suits!"

Mother hastily ran out to fetch the culprits back and

the two of them had their seats slapped, not so much in punishment as to repair the damage done. But Francie stuck out his tongue when he passed Michael and said: "Dirty sneak! It's glad I am I hid your books in the barn!"

"Mother! Did ye hear what Francie's after saying?" cried Michael indignantly. "It's in the barn he put me books, the rapscallion! Wait till I lay me hands on him, he'll be sorry yet for his diviltry!" With eyes rolling threateningly in Francie's direction, Michael rushed to the barn where indeed he found his satchel with the books and they much the worse for damp and dust and the teeth of inquisitive mice.

"It's your own fault," said Mother. "You should have looked after your things better. Sure you know by now that the twins aren't to be trusted, and they little boys without sense. You're old enough to mind your own property. It's a poor hen that can't scratch for itself." Michael had to be content with that, though small comfort it was to him.

Brigid was not slovenly like Michael. Her school things were neatly packed in a hat box which she kept under the bed, and no one dared touch the box for fear of her anger.

Bran felt that something exciting was going to happen. He ran up and down barking loudly and Mother told Michael to lock him in the barn or he'd be sure to follow the children to school.

77

Liam could hardly part from his mother. He clung to her neck as though it was the last time he would ever see her. She had to shove him away, saying good-humoredly: "Go along with ye, boy, and what ails ye? Sure, ye'll be back before dinner, please God! Run off and be a man now." And, going into the house, she shook her head, thinking of the difference between the twins. Liam so fine and hearty and yet so sweet and tender, Francie crippled and delicate and yet so bold and independent. She smiled and cried a little as she washed the dishes, missing her babies for all her brave talk of peace.

Francie indeed did not waste sentiment on his first day of leaving home. He had cut himself a stick and walked with as much of a swagger as his lame foot would allow, pretending to himself that it was no new thing at all to be going to school and that he was bored stiff with it already. Liam, however, clung to Michael and Brigid, asking them hundreds of questions about the school and the mistress.

"Sure, ye needn't be frightened, Liam," said Brigid. "We're all together in a big room, ye know, and Michael'll take care no harm comes to ye."

"And the mistress'll be good and kind to ye," added Michael.

Liam was pleased but Francie said grandly: "It's a pity we've a woman teacher. I'd rather have a master meself."

When they approached the little whitewashed schoolhouse with *Scoil,* which is Irish for school, written above the door, and when they saw all the children walking into it, in number more than twice the fingers on your hand, even Francie felt awed and put his hand into Bridy's.

It was indeed a nice teacher who received the twins when they were shyly introduced by Michael. There were several other new boys and girls to shake hands with her and the old ones all wanted her attention, so it was not to be wondered at that she got a bit mixed up and put Francie and Liam far apart on different benches.

Liam's lip quivered when he saw this but Francie bravely marched up to the teacher and said: "Please, Miss Reilly, I want to sit beside Liam." The teacher looked puzzled, for she had not got hold of the names yet. Michael had to come to the rescue and explain. The teacher apologized kindly and put the twins together, so that Francie began to think highly of her.

"For a woman she is not bad," he whispered to Liam. "She understands a man's feelings."

"She is a darling," said Liam fervently. "When I'm grown up, I'll marry her." And he gazed contentedly at the teacher.

"Arra, you're always thinking of getting married," Francie whispered disdainfully. "Meself 'll be a bachelor, like the gamekeeper up at the castle and he with shining guns and big boots an' all, an' no women to mind him!" The teacher here put a stop to their conversation by telling them that speaking was not allowed unless they were asked to do so.

The schoolroom was wide and low, with a few pictures on the wall, some flowerpots in the window, and many dark, stained and scratched benches. The children were divided into a group of big ones, who were able to do work all by themselves if the teacher wrote an exercise for them on the board, and small ones, who had to be minded and taught all the time, some saying the alphabet and others reading out of a book. But the first day there were many things to be attended to, apart from teaching. The children had to show their books and the work they had done at home, and the teacher had to write down the list of new children, with their ages.

Poor Michael felt ashamed when he came to show his frazzled books and Miss Reilly asked him what had happened to them. She looked angry and Michael would fain have excused himself if he had been able to do so without accusing Francie. That was impossible, so he mutely traced circles on the clay floor with his big toe.

Francie looked on with startled eyes, uncertain whether he would be allowed to speak up.

"Well, Michael, I'm disappointed in you," said the teacher sadly. "You'd be my best pupil if it wasn't for your slovenliness. I'll have to cure you once and for all, so I'll keep ye in at recess today and tomorrow."

Michael looked crestfallen and Francie threw all scruples to the winds and cried out: "It's not Michael's fault at all, at all. It's meself spoilt his books an' hid them in the barn!" There was a roar of laughter from the other children, and Francie sat down again as red as a poppy.

Teacher's mouth twitched a little as she answered: "That's a good boy to speak up for your brother, and I'm right glad to hear it was not Michael's fault this time, though he should have put the books where no little fingers could reach them. I'll forgive ye this time, Michael," she added. "But don't let it happen again." Michael went to his seat, well pleased with his brother and his teacher both.

When all the children had had their turn showing their work and giving their names, Miss Reilly said she was going to make an occasion of the first day by telling a story.

"Hooray!" cried the children, and looked at each other with shining eyes. The twins cocked their ears and Liam fixed his soft brown eyes on the teacher with flattering interest.

"It's about a holy man I'm going to tell ye," she said. "His name was Francis."

"That's me own name!" cried Francie, forgetting instructions. The children tittered and the teacher showed Francie how he must lift his finger when he wanted to say something. Francie thought it a great novelty and intended to practice it. Miss Reilly continued:

"Saint Francis was especially fond of animals. He would step out of his little bit of a hut in the mornings and talk to the birds as though they were Christians. 'Where are me little friends, the sparrows, today?' he'd say in a coaxing voice. 'Is it up in the tree tops they are, talking scandal to their neighbors? Or are they minding their business, giving thanks to their Maker, as they should?'

"He would stretch out his hand and down would come the sparrows, listening to his words with their heads to one side, their eyes like dewdrops. Saint Francis would share his crusts of bread with them and stroke their feathers, telling them that they should be grateful to God.

" 'Who is it gave you the trees with branches to swing on and the blue sky above?' he'd say. 'Isn't it Our Lord Himself whom we should praise and glorify to the end of our days?'

"Many other birds would come fluttering down to him, perching on his head and shoulders and peeking into his pockets for crumbs. And sometimes Saint Francis would scold them. He once told the raven he had no call to be taking all the glittering things he could find and to be hiding them in his nest. But when the raven looked crushed with guilt, he buttered him up by praising his shining black coat.

"But it was not only the innocent creatures that would come to Saint Francis! Once, when a man-eating wolf roamed in the neighborhood of a city frightening the inhabitants, Saint Francis went out to meet the creature, hoping to stop his bloodshed. The wolf ran at him with open jaws, ready to attack him, but no sooner had the saint made the sign of the cross than the wolf shut his jaws and laid himself down at Saint Francis's feet.

" 'Brother wolf,' said Saint Francis, 'it is sorry I am indeed to hear such tales of you. There's not a man in the city that has a good word for you. Wouldn't it be better to be at peace with the world than to have to be hiding everywhere for fear of the anger of others? If I now make the peace between you and your enemies, will you promise to behave better in future?'

"The wolf bowed his head and showed with eyes and tail that he agreed. Saint Francis went back to the city with the wolf by his side as meek as a lamb, so that the people were amazed to see it. Saint Francis took the wolf to the marketplace where the people all flocked together and there he assured them that they would remain unmolested if they would agree to feed the wolf to the end of his days. The people gladly promised and then Saint Francis said to the wolf: 'Brother wolf, now you must pledge yourself never to hurt man or beast again.' Thereupon the fierce animal lifted his paw and placed it in the hand of Saint Francis. From that day on the wolf never harmed a mortal. He became the gentlest of creatures, going from door to door to beg his food. When at last he died of old age, there wasn't a person in the town that was not sorry. So you see, Saint Francis could change even a wild animal just because he loved every creature that God has made."

There was a deep silence when the teacher had finished speaking, but Francie put up his finger.

"Well, and what is it you want?"

"Please, miss," asked Francie timidly. "Did Saint Francis love jellyfish an' spiders?" Some children giggled.

"Well," said the teacher. "I was not thinking of those animals but I suppose a holy man would love them all." She could not suppress a little shudder, for she herself particularly disliked spiders.

"I suppose he could *love* them if he tried very hard," said Francie pensively. "But could he talk to them?"

The teacher smiled. "Saint Francis lived a long time ago," she said. "Maybe it has been so long since anyone loved spiders and jellyfish that they have grown disappointed and unfriendly." The children thought this very likely and were satisfied with the explanation.

"Are ye fond of dogs, miss?" asked Michael hopefully, thinking he might persuade the teacher to let Bran join the class. Miss Reilly had scarcely said that she was very fond of them when a loud noise startled them all. A flowerpot crashed to the floor, bursting into smithereens as Bran jumped through the open window and landed on Michael's lap, causing a great commotion in the class. Every-

one shouted at once. Some children helped the teacher gather the scattered fragments of the flowerpot and sweep up the plant which had been hopelessly bruised, others stood on their benches to have a better peep at Bran, and some of the bolder ones began to run and dance around the room shouting with glee. Bran was very elated at having found his master and celebrated the occasion with loud barks, jumping out of Michael's arms and running about frantically. At last Michael and Brigid persuaded him to lie down and the teacher rapped with her pencil on the desk calling the children to order.

"Whose dog is this?" she asked sternly. Michael timidly admitted that it was his.

"Well, don't let this happen again," she said. "A school is no place for dogs, and it's one of our best plants he's ruined. I'm afraid I will have to ask you to bring back a shilling tomorrow to pay for another one. We can't all be suffering from your dog's diviltry." A whole shilling! Michael and Brigid looked at each other with open mouths. Wherever were they going to get that from! But they only bowed their heads and Michael said he was sorry.

"Well, you'd better be going home now with the creature," said Miss Reilly. "I doubt if we'll get him off any other way and it'll soon be time."

So Michael was let off and ran home with Bran, oppressed with misgivings about the shilling. Mother was surprised when she saw him and angry with Bran when she heard all. She went into the yard to consult Father, who was doing odd jobs about the place until his ankle got well enough for him to resume heavier work. Father came in looking very grave and, when Michael told him about the shilling, he shook his head and sighed.

"It's a deal of money we've lost through this accident of mine and every penny is riches to us," he said. "I see it was all the fault of the dog and I know ye've set your heart on him, so I'll pay it this time, but if he goes on costing us money, he'll have to be sent to Farmer Flynn."

"Oh, Father, it's sorry I am it happened, indeed, and I will try to take better care of Bran, and I do thank ye for the shilling. I will try and help to earn it back. Couldn't I pick berries for you, Mother? Heaps and heaps of them so you can make jelly for the whole winter?"

Mother smiled. "That would be a help," she agreed.

The first one to come home after Michael was Liam, who had run so hard that he staggered into the kitchen all flushed and breathless.

"What is it? What's the matter?" cried Mother anxiously. "Did anything happen?" Liam flung his arms round her neck and said: "I ran to be home soon so you wouldn't worry!"

"Bless ye, boy!" cried Mother. "It was your coming so early that gave me a fright." She kissed him heartily. "And where is Francie?" she asked.

"Francie's gone footballing with the other boys."

"Footballing! With his foot!"

"He said he could run as well as any."

"Well, I hope he won't kill himself," said Mother.

Brigid wandered in presently with long tales about the school and how all the girls had admired Bran and what a pity it was about the lovely plant that was just starting to bloom. "Ye're a naughty dog and no mistake," she told Bran, patting him lightly on the head.

As it grew later and later there was still no Francie. Mother glanced at the clock ever so often and at last she asked Michael to go and look for him. "Something may have happened to him. Boys do be so wild when they're playing, and him with his crippled foot. Please, Michael, go and fetch him!"

Michael went and Mother counted the minutes until he came back, saying little prayers for her young son's safety. At last she saw the two through the window, Michael marching like a policeman and dragging poor Francie along with him.

Mother thanked Michael for his trouble but Francie gave him an indignant look and stepped up to his mother, planting both hands on his hips.

"Ye shouldn't be making a fool of me before the other fellows," he said. "A man can play games after school, can't he, without having the whole of his family come an' fetch him!" And Francie turned on his heels with a proud toss of his head. Mother took the rebuke meekly, but the corners of her mouth twitched a little.

"Did you ever see the like of those children?" she asked.

FIVE

Picking Blackberries

THE next morning at breakfast Father gave Michael the shilling for Miss Reilly. Michael took it remorsefully. "I'll earn it back for you, see if I won't!" he promised.

Liam swallowed a large mouthful of stirabout and spoke up hastily: "I can help ye. I've a whole penny, I have!"

"How did ye get that?" Mother asked suspiciously.

"I found it," said Liam.

"Where did ye find it?"

"On the floor there, in that corner." Liam pointed to the dark place beside the chimney.

"Then it is mine," said Mother. "I must have dropped it when I gave Brigid money for the milk yesterday."

"It isn't yours," Liam protested. "How can it be yours when it's meself that found it? Maybe the fairies put it there for me." His face brightened.

"Well, ye may give it to Michael now, if ye like," said Mother. "But next time ye find something, I'd like to know about it or I'll begin to think it's not good fairies at all we have in this house but very wicked ones!"

Liam gravely emptied his pockets, putting his treasures one by one on the table. A piece of cork, a few nuts, a glass bead, a dead beetle, an old crust of bread, a matchbox, a pink pebble, and, at last, the penny. Father and Mother looked at each other and laughed.

"No wonder I have to be sewing up your pockets all the time if that's the way you use them!" cried Brigid indignantly.

"Well, what else are pockets for?" said Francie, speaking up for his brother.

Mother was examining Liam's treasures and held up

the moldy bread, sniffing at it. "What's that for, may I ask?"

"Oh," said Liam carelessly. "I put that into me pocket in case I see a dog or a rabbit dying with hunger by the roadside. An' then again it will be handy if I get lost meself. There's hundreds of reasons why I keep this crust." Taking it out of his mother's hand he stuffed it back into his pocket. "When the English are at us again, they won't starve *me*," he added proudly.

"Sure, an' that wouldn't be enough," argued Francie.

"It would be a start," said Liam.

"Well, and what's this here?" asked Mother, taking up the matchbox and opening it. But she let it fall with a yell, for a big hairy spider jumped out and scurried over her apron to the floor. Liam gave a wail and jumped from his chair.

"Patsy!" he cried. "Me spider!" He ran after it only to see it disappear into a crack in the wall. Crouching down he peered into the black opening. "Patsy! Patsy!" he called in his most coaxing voice, as though the insect were a chicken or a cat. "Won't ye come back to Liam?" But the spider refused to reappear. No doubt it had an anxious family somewhere. Liam sobbed, and Mother felt sorry for him.

"I didn't know ye had a pet in there, son," she said,

frowning at Michael and Brigid, who found it difficult to keep serious faces.

"Didn't I tell ye it would be no use?" whispered Francie, throwing a consoling arm around his twin brother. "It's wasted on them spiders, so it is!"

"But she was just getting used to me," said Liam sadly. "I saw her smile once. If only I had her a little longer!" He burst into fresh tears.

Mother looked puzzled. "What's it all about?" she asked.

"Och, Mother," explained Francie. "It is all because of Saint Francis an' him loving the animals as the teacher told us. I asked her about spiders an' the like, an' she said maybe they'd be nicer if someone loved 'em an' so Liam here has been doing nothing but sleuthering this spider he caught. But I told him it's no use, they're past mending." Francie took a deep breath after his long speech, throwing an angry glance at Michael and Brigid, who were now laughing outright.

Mother herself could hardly restrain a smile, and Father said: "Come here, Liam. Come and sit on my knee." Liam gladly mounted that place of honor and Father continued: "What would you do if a great big giant took ye away from here and locked ye up in a dark box?"

Liam thought it over carefully. "I would bite a hole in

it an' then I would run home as soon as ever I could!" he cried.

Father smiled and pinched Liam's ear. "That's exactly what your spider is after doing, son," he said. Liam looked confused.

"But spiders have no homes an' no families. I know, 'cause I've seen 'em hundreds of times an' they sitting all alone in their sticky webs!"

"Well, that's their life, son, and we can't judge. Maybe that's as good to them as a fireplace is to us. But you'd better be going to school now or the doors'll be shut!" Father pointed to the clock. It was true. The children hastily picked up their parcels and scrambled off, leaving the kitchen very quiet and Bran very lonely. The dog understood that he was not to follow the children—Michael had made that clear—so he resigned himself, lying down in front of the fire, his muzzle on his forepaws, yawning now and then to show how bored he was.

Michael was firmly resolved to pay back that shilling to his parents by picking blackberries, but he had to wait till Saturday. After school there were too many things to be done about the house to allow him to take time off. Brigid and the twins had promised to help him. Michael said he'd be glad if his sister came with him, though he didn't want the twins because they would only be in the way.

97

Early Saturday morning Michael and his sister set off with huge baskets on their arms, bread in their pockets, and Bran running around them in circles, barking his delight. The twins watched them from the doorway with a reproachful look on their chubby faces. It was one of those beautifully clear days that are so rare in Ireland, and usually have to be admired through grimy school windows. The sky was deep blue and the leaves on the trees glowed in rich autumn colors. Michael chose the way through the woods; he said he knew a nice place for blackberries in the meadows beyond. The children's footsteps rustled on the leaf-covered wood paths and the huge trees creaked and sighed over their heads, seeming to say:

> "We sing a song of a wood that grieves
>   When the chill winds blow,
> To tear away from our arms the leaves
>   In their autumn glow.
>
> "A gusty wind bears them off; they rise
>   With a whirl and sweep,
> Like flaming birds they assail the skies,
>   Leaving us to weep.

"They curve and swerve in their fluttering flight,
   Seeking where to rest.
Then, faltering faintly, they slowly 'light
   On earth's soft breast.

"We sing a song of a wood that grieves
   When the sun turns cold
And trees will sigh over wandering leaves
   As the year grows old."

"Will ye look at those lovely toadstools!" cried Brigid, pointing to a group of bright-colored fungi. The wood was full of them, some long and graceful with gray hoods like umbrellas, others white with a bad smell and black tips or with thick bulbous stems. Michael, who had learned a little botany from the teacher, explained that the latter were poisonous.

"Ye can tell the wicked ones by the look of them," he added, pointing to a huge toadstool with a fat purple hood and a huge bulbous scarlet stem streaked with green. It looked fantastic and Brigid couldn't help shivering. She believed that each toadstool had its own particular fairy, and she thought it must be a bad one that belonged to such a bloody-looking thing. Perhaps he was a little crooked man with a hump on his back and a big red nose and black eyes. All around, the gnarled moss-covered tree trunks seemed to be sheltering millions of such creatures. She could almost hear them sniggering in their hiding places and she suddenly longed for the sunny open fields.

"I'm for hurrying," she said. "We'll never get our berries this way!" So they did hurry and were soon standing in the friendly meadow where many straggling bramble bushes promised a rich harvest. They set to work immediately, and for a while there was no sound except the dropping of berries in the baskets, the grunts and barks of Bran digging out a rabbit hole, and the humming of insects. There were plenty of berries, and now and again the children could not resist putting a large one into their mouths but they agreed that they should count them and the one that had eaten least in the end would win.

"How many have ye eaten now?" asked Brigid, stopping to suck a finger that had been pricked by a thorn.

"Ten, and you?"

"I've only had six, so I can take three more and still be winning!" cried Brigid joyfully, popping a plump one into her mouth.

Michael had a hankering after the berries that were out of his reach. However juicy the ones on the lower branches might be, none seemed so luscious as those up high, and he felt he must get them. With his knife he cut himself a big forked stick with which he tried to coax down some of the higher branches. He lost his balance and tumbled right

into the prickly bush, tearing his clothes and scratching his face and hands.

"I'll have them yct, you wait!" he cried angrily when he saw Brigid's laughing face, and he resumed his efforts with the stick until he had captured some of the berries. But alas! They turned out to be far less gorgeous than they had appeared from below. Brigid giggled.

"Aren't you the clever one! Look at all I picked down here, but boys will be wasting their time on what they can't get." In her hurry to add another big juicy one to her collection, Brigid ran her face full into a sticky cobweb. It was the worst that could happen to her. She danced up and down crying: "Oh, dear! Oh, dear! It's in me neck! It's creeping down this minute!" until Michael assured her there was no spider though he had examined every fold in her dress.

"I hate spiders," said Brigid when she dared to believe all was well and again breathed freely. "Wherever the berries are round and fat and shiny, there's sure to be a sticky web in front of them with the mean creature in the middle looking at ye as if he was daring ye to come on!" Brigid shuddered.

"Where's Bran?" cried Michael, missing the dog. The children looked around.

103

"There he is! Oh, Michael!" Brigid clutched her brother's arm in terror. "He's after rousing Mr. Sheehy's bull."

Indeed, Bran, tired of rabbit holes, had frisked over to the huge new bull of Farmer Sheehy and was circling around him barking loudly. Now bulls are not cows, as everyone knows, and they don't have the patience of cows. This bull had just been separated from his family and put into a straw-covered cart to be jolted for miles along dusty roads with nothing to drink. Now he was locked up

104

all alone in a meadow and, weary and cross, he felt in no mood to be barked at by an impudent puppy. He rose slowly, shook his thick head, and pawed the ground. Bran was undaunted and snapped at his tail.

"Will ye come here, Bran! Here, bold dog!" cried the children, hoarse with fear. But Bran didn't know the danger he was in until the bull lowered his horns and made a sudden charge. Then the dog gave a yelp of dismay and went head over heels in his hurry to be off.

"He's coming here! Quick! Into the bushes!" shouted Michael who saw what would happen. Brigid was too frightened to pay heed and dashed across the open meadow in the hope of reaching the wall at the end. Distracted by the flap of her red skirt, the bull lurched around, rolling his bloodshot eyes. Then, with a bellow of rage, he plunged after her.

"Help! Help! Mother! Michael!" cried poor Brigid, making an effort to run faster though her heart was pounding in her throat and her lungs felt ready to burst. Never would she forget that dreadful moment when she seemed to feel the breath of the mad creature on her neck. Shutting her eyes tightly, she gave herself up for lost. But not for nothing did she have a bold, gallant brother. How could Michael stand there and see his sister gored to death before his eyes? He leaped after the bull and aimed his forked stick like a spear, driving the points into the animal's hide. The bull stopped and turned around.

"Run, Bridy!" Michael cried. "Run for your life!" And the brave boy waited a second to be sure his sister was on her way to safety. Then, as the bull lunged at him with lowered head, he leaped aside just in time to escape the sharp horns. A mad chase followed, watched anxiously from behind the wall by Brigid and Bran. Michael managed to dodge the ponderous bull again and again, and the creature grew angrier every time the nimble boy skipped out of his reach. At last Michael took refuge behind a fat tree and the two went round and round it, the bull bellowing and snorting frightfully and Michael with his eyes on the wall.

"Wave your skirt!" he cried desperately, for the perspiration was streaming down his face and he felt so exhausted he could hardly breathe. Luckily Brigid understood and she stepped out of her skirt and waved it over the wall, screeching at the top of her voice the while. For a moment the bull turned his head but that was time enough for Michael. Across the field he flew and then over the wall in the nick of time for a horn of the pursuing beast grazed the calf of his leg as he leaped.

106

"I'm done for!" he gasped, sinking to the ground on the other side. Now it was Brigid's turn to be active. She scrambled down some rocks and found a spring in which she wetted her kerchief. Then she bathed poor Michael's throbbing head until the boy felt better and was able to get up again, though his legs still trembled under him.

"Thanks be to God! Ye had a hard time of it! I don't know how ye escaped him," said Brigid. "Yes, me bold Bran, look at that for ye! Ye've all but kilt us both. Will ye behave better now in future?" Bran promised faithfully with limpid brown eyes, so the children forgave him.

"But the berries!" cried Michael. "We've left them in the field!"

That was a fix! Brigid peeped over the wall and a snort warned her that the bull was still in the neighborhood. Like all creatures who get angry, he suffered most himself and he had laid himself down, quivering all over, covered with foam and probably with a splitting headache. When his bleary, bloodshot eye detected Brigid, he made a movement as if to get up. But that was enough. She ducked her head swiftly.

"Isn't it the pity of the world we didn't think of bringing the baskets?" she asked with a sigh.

"No, if we'd taken them, it's likely we'd not have got away," said Michael, shuddering at the thought of the danger they had both been in. Ever so often neighbors would tell of accidents happening to people because of angry bulls. "But I'll do me best to get them back," he added. "If you'll stay here, I'll see what can be done." Michael ran off into the woods, hoping to be able to reach the abandoned baskets without attracting the bull's attention. If he had not been so bent on paying back that shilling to his father, he would never have ventured into the meadow again. His heart hammered in his breast as he slid down through the brushwood and stood on the soft grass. A swift look, a couple of jumps, and he was back safe with both baskets in his hands. The bull had not even so much as looked round; he was too far off to hear anything and too much spent to care.

"I've got them!" cried Michael, waving the baskets. Brigid had been awaiting him anxiously.

"Thanks be to God," she said. "I don't see how ye *dared* to go back!" Michael smiled. After all, she was a girl, and there was no need to tell her that he wondered at it himself.

"Are ye as starved with the hunger as I am?" he asked, suddenly aware of a gnawing sensation in the middle of his stomach that was *not* fear. Brigid nodded her head vigorously, her reddish gold curls flopping about.

"Well then, I'm for having some of this bread." Michael pulled out of his pockets the squashed remains of what had been meant for their lunch. It tasted just as good as if it had come straight from the loaf—better in fact, for hadn't the children just been snatched from the very jaws of death? They might never have had another taste of good homemade bread! Bran, of course, got his share, though he did not deserve it.

"We must fill our baskets," said Michael, when all the bread had been eaten, "or it will all have been for nothing!" They rambled up the hills to be well away from the bull, and gathered berries from wherever they happened to grow, high shrubs, low creepers, or hedges. After a while Brigid felt tired and sat down to rest herself, leaving the indefatigable Michael to add the last berries to the baskets, which were nearly full. She had a grand view from the rock on which she was sitting; she could see the village and the bay with its green islands and, beyond, the silver streak of the ocean. The salt wind brushed her cheeks and played with her curls and the murmur of the sea was in her ears. Somehow it seemed very good to be alive. Bran, who had laid himself beside her, must have felt the same, for he looked up and licked her hand.

"Bridy! Bridy! Will ye look at this!" That was Michael's voice and it sounded excited. Brigid jumped up and ran to join him.

109

"What's up?" she asked, and then stood with open mouth. Part of the rock on which she had been sitting rose sheer into the air and the weeds growing on top fell over and covered the sides. Michael had pushed some of these aside and revealed a deep mysterious cave. The children crawled inside but the dog would not go in. He whined and ran about, nosing the ground. It was a beautiful cave, very roomy with lots of nooks and crevices and soft sand on the ground. It extended further than the children cared to go without a light. Michael examined the walls, which were irregular and dark with age.

"There is something written here," he said. "Come and look." He was peering at the crooked letters that were carved into the rocky wall.

"NI BUAIREAS TASC NA TUAIRISC AIR," he read, for the children had learned Irish at school. "It means: 'I have not heard from him either living or dead,' doesn't it?"

"It looks as though people have been here before," said Brigid thoughtfully. "They are old letters too. Do ye see any more of them?" Michael was looking carefully at walls and ceiling in the hope of finding another clue.

"Aye, this here." Michael was on his knees before a few scribbled letters low down on the same wall.

"IS DONA AN RUD A T-OCRAS ACH IS MEASA AN RUD AN TART," he read. "Hunger is a bad thing but thirst is worse."

110

"There is a name under it," cried Brigid, crouching beside him. "It's so small I can hardly see it. Can you make it out, Michael?"

"I can, so," said he. "This here is a 'P,' and then there is an 'M' and an 'E.' "

"Oh, Micky!" exclaimed Brigid. "It's P. McEgan—ye don't think—it couldn't be . . ."

"Ye mean Gorrane's son? Ye have it right, I think—wasn't his name Patrick?"

"There may have been other McEgans."

"But—look at that for ye—there's a date here. See! 1601."

"SIXTEEN HUNDRED AND ONE. . . ." Brigid stared awestruck at the inscription. "So long ago." The children were silent for a moment as though listening for the whirring wings of Time. "Then it *is* Gorrane's cave," said Brigid at last with a deep sigh.

"And it's ours now," Michael added with a grin. "I'm going to put our name over Patrick's." He took out his knife, scratching into the rocky wall the words:

M. AND B. O'SULLIVAN 1930

The children were full of their discovery, and could talk of nothing else on the way home. "I'm for keeping the cave a secret," said Brigid. "Ye know what'll happen if

111

we tell anyone. The whole village will be here and it won't be any fun at all."

"That's a fact," said Michael. "I was thinking the same thing meself. We'll have this a secret just between us and it'll be bad luck to betray it."

"Shake hands on it," said Brigid, and the two solemnly shook hands.

That evening, around the fire, Father, Mother, and the twins were kept spellbound by the tale of Brigid's and Michael's escape from the bull. When Mother heard the mischief Bran had nearly done that day, she shuddered, taking Brigid into her arms and covering her with kisses.

"Oh, that dog!" she said. "Why did ye ever bring him here!" Father praised Michael for his presence of mind. "God bless ye, Micky. Ye've been a brave boy and I'm proud of ye," he said.

"Oh, but I *was* afraid, Father," faltered Michael honestly. "As soon as I could think, I was. It all happened so quickly there was no time to be doing anything but run for me life!"

"Arra, why didn't ye fight the beast!" cried Francie. "I would have taken me gun an' shot him dead." Using his father's oak stick, Francie so effectively showed what he would have done, that he nearly poked his mother's eyes out.

"And then ye'd have had to pay fifty pounds for the bull, laddo," said Father. "No, ye did very well, Michael, and Mother and I are ever so grateful to ye, aren't we, Mother?" Such high praise from Father made Michael blush to the tips of his ears.

SIX

What Happened to the Twins?

"WHERE are the twins?" asked Mother on Sunday morning, putting on her shawl in front of the little mirror. She couldn't wear her hat, for Bran had chewed all the ribbons off it. "I had them spick and span awhile ago—have they run out on me? Go and look, Bridy. We'll be off to church in a minute."

"Francie! Liam!" cried Brigid. They came running into the kitchen and Mother saw nothing amiss with their costume until they turned to get their caps.

114

"Will ye look at that!" she cried and Michael, Father, and Brigid all began to laugh.

"What's up?" asked Francie suspiciously. He looked at his shoes; they were shining. His suit was clean, but his hands! Ah, well, what can you expect? He frowned. "What ails ye all? C'm' on, Liam." Liam threw an uneasy glance at the merry faces behind him.

"Ye've been sliding from that rock again, haven't ye now?" Mother said sternly.

"Maybe we have," Liam admitted.

"And ye did it more than a dozen times," Mother continued.

"Maybe we did," nodded Francie. "But where's the harm?"

"Arra, your breeches are through!" cried Brigid.

Francie hastily felt the seat of his pants and found his shirt sticking through a hole. He blushed. "Let me see yours, Liam." He burst into laughter at the sight of his twin brother.

"Go and change, both of you. Ye'll have to put on your school breeches," said Mother, and Brigid sighed, thinking of all the darning she would have to do that week.

They were late at church and the family had to find places where they could. Francie and Liam wriggled to the front and found a nice seat near the altar. Mother did not mind their sitting apart, for they always behaved well in church. They each had a little prayer book full of colored pictures and they enjoyed looking at these during the service. There was one picture they liked best, that of little Jesus standing sweet and straight in His white tunic among the bearded old men in the temple. Francie tried to imagine what it would have been like to have Jesus to play with. He knew that Our Lord had been a child like himself, but somehow he could not imagine Him soiling that spotless white tunic of His. Would Mother Mary have given Him a darker suit sometimes? Francie hoped so, for it is hard to play properly and keep clean. He felt it must have been very difficult for Our Lord to be perfect as a boy. There always seems to be so much mischief lying around which one cannot help falling into when one is young. Later, of course, it would be easy enough. Grown people are naturally virtuous. Francie had the greatest admiration for the Child Jesus. So had Liam. They both wished very much to be like Him and Francie resolved he would try it at least for one day.

When Mass was over, Mother and Father stood talking to some friends who asked them to come and pay them a visit in the afternoon. Sunday was Mother's day off. She had no cooking to do, for the dinner was prepared on Saturday to be eaten at noon on Sunday, and after that Mother was free to do what she liked. She and Father gladly accepted the invitation, but they couldn't stay long talking for the children were hungry and begged them to return home. They knew that a delicious lamb stew was waiting for them by the side of the fire.

Alas! When they reached home, a sad spectacle met their eyes. Michael had tied Bran to a leg of the kitchen table before he went to church to make sure he would do no mischief, but the dog had chewed through the string. Thus having gained his liberty, he had looked about for something to eat. There was a good smell from the pot by the fire and since he could not lift the lid, the dog had upset the pot, spilling the lovely stew all over the flagstones. Bran knew very well he had done wrong. He cowered in the corner and whimpered and didn't look at all surprised when Mother took him up and gave him a few angry slaps.

"You bold unbiddable creature!" she cried, indignantly. "Now ye're after spoiling our dinner on us! And there's hardly any bread even in the house! It's nothing but botheration you've brought us and I'll have ye sent away this day to Farmer Flynn's." She had hardly said the words when Francie and Liam clung sobbing to her skirts and Michael and Brigid both fell on their pet, hugging him and begging Mother not to send him off.

"He'll be good—he's a good dog, really," cried Brigid. "Sure, he meant no harm."

And Michael said: "It was me own fault. I should have known he would chew through that string."

"See what trouble that dog has brought us," said Father, looking ruefully into the pot, which was all but empty, and sniffing hungrily the rich smell of the overturned stew. "First it's breaking flowerpots and spoiling hats and chasing chickens, then he nearly has both of you kilt by a bull, and now it's our dinner on the flagstones. Whatever do ye expect us to do? Smile and be happy? There, Michael, sweep up this stew and give it to the pigs."

120

"I'll have to be cooking all evening instead of drinking tea with Nancy Coogan, and all on account of that rapscallion!" said Mother.

"No, Mother darling, I'll take care ye can go out if ye'll let us keep Bran a little longer!" begged Brigid. "I can cook a meal for ye. Michael will help me."

"I'll help ye meself," said Francie, feeling that now was the time to carry out the morning's resolution. "I'll do everything for ye, Mother, leave it all to me." Mother kissed him.

"Well, Bridy, if ye will do it, I'll be grateful," she said. "It's a long time since I had a talk with poor Nancy. Ye don't need to be cooking a lot, ye know."

"And may we keep the dog?" asked Michael.

"We'll see," said Mother. "He'll have to be very good, for there isn't much more I'll stand from him."

So it was arranged and after they had eaten a scant meal of bread and tea and Father had smoked his pipe and read his paper, he and Mother went out, leaving the children to take care of the housework. Brigid felt that she was boss now, being the only woman. She looked around the kitchen like a general surveying a battlefield, wondering where to attack first.

"The twins can wash up the dishes," she said. "Michael, you get me some potatoes out of the garden and some turf for the fire. I'm going to tidy up and then I'll make scones," and Brigid tied a big apron under her chin.

The twins were very proud of the trust placed in them, but there was a short dispute as to who should wash and who should dry.

"Look at this elegant towel," said Francie. "Drying is *much* more fun but I'll let you do it, Liam, you're so good at it."

Liam happily accepted the lesser task of drying and Francie became master of the dishpan. They washed up very nicely, breaking only two cups, and that was Bran's fault because he walked right in front of Liam, who was carrying them to the cupboard. Also, there was a telltale pool of soapy water under Francie's feet, but no one should mind trifles like that.

"It was great good luck for ye to have us help ye, wasn't it?" said Francie, clasping his hands behind his back and admiring the clean crockery which Liam had piled on the dresser. "You'd never have got finished without us, would ye now? Come on, Liam, we'll give Bran an airing." The twins ran off, to Brigid's relief.

"At last we can work in peace," she said to Michael. She had swept the floor and tidied the bedroom. Now she rolled out some dough, made of sour milk, flour, and baking soda, and fashioned it into scones. She asked

Michael to hand her the big pot. When the scones were shaped, Brigid put them on the bottom of the pot and hung it on the hook over the fire. Then she put the lid on and Michael picked some nice glowing coals of peat out of the fire for her and arranged them on the lid. So the pot became an oven and the scones could be left to bake.

"We'll make the place look fine for Mother," said Brigid, feeling her importance as a housewife. "You stick the praties into the ashes to roast. I'm going to shine the

123

pots and pans." Brigid fetched her scouring brushes and white sand and made all the iron and pewter in the kitchen gleam like silver.

"Your scones smell good," said Michael, who crouched before the fire watching his potatoes. "Do ye think they are done?"

Brigid looked at the clock. "Another five minutes," she said. "You ready the table, Micky, and I'll be finishing off the scones and putting on the kettle."

"Where are the twins? I haven't seen them this long while."

"Nor I," said Brigid, looking out of the window. "They'll be around somewhere. They never go far. Like as not they've gone to meet Mother and Father. But look at the sky! It's going to rain in a minute!" Michael came over to the window.

"That's a thunderstorm," he said, watching the white heads pile up on the purple clouds. "There, what did I tell ye!" An ominous rumble in the sky confirmed his words. "Here are Father and Mother, thanks be to God! Just in time!" And the children ran to fetch them in. They had hardly shut the door behind them when a thunderclap shook the house and the rain started to pour down.

"Did ye ever see the like of that weather!" cried Mother.

"I hope you are all safe inside—where are Francie and Liam?" Mother's watchful eyes missed them at once.

"We thought they'd gone to meet you," explained Michael. "They went out to play and we haven't seen them since. They're sure to be somewhere near."

"Well, they ought to come in," said Mother. "You fetch them, Michael. I wonder they don't have the sense to come in of themselves. My! Brigid, ye have spoilt us. Scones! Child, they're lovely!" Michael waited a minute in the hope of getting praise for his potatoes, though he didn't deserve any for half of them were badly scorched. Mother, however, motioned to him to go and fetch her babies, so he threw a coat over his shoulders and went out into the rain.

"Francie! Liam!" he called. "Francie! Liam!" There was no answer. "Bother them," he grumbled, plodding barefooted through the muddy yard. He looked into the barn, the kitchen garden, the hay loft, and down the road, but without success. "Wherever can they be?" he wondered, frowning. Above his head two armies of clouds were battling each other. Fierce rumbling followed each piercing flash of lightning. Michael soon was drenched to the skin and hurried back to the warm, dry kitchen. As he opened the door a gust of wind whirled through so that he could hardly shut it again.

125

"I can't find them," he said. "They're nowhere about." Father and Mother sat at the table enjoying Brigid's food.

"They'll be sheltering with the neighbors," said Father peacefully, taking a big bite out of a scone. "They'll soon get hungry and come home for their food."

"But they'll be so wet!" cried Mother. "And Francie does be coughing in weather like this!"

"Well, wait till I've finished me dinner and if they're not here yet I'll go for them." The rain continued to beat against the windowpanes but the thunder died away only to break out anew some time later. Still there were no twins to be seen.

"Well, I'll go for them," said Father, who saw that Mother was getting very anxious. "Hand me my coat, Michael."

"I'll go with ye," said Michael. "Perhaps they are at Mrs. O'Flaherty's!" The two went up the road to the widow's cottage.

In the meantime Mother and Brigid waited anxiously in the dark kitchen, lit up from time to time by flashes of lightning. Each time the heavy thunder rumbled over the house they winced.

"If they weren't so bold, I'd feel easier in me mind," said Mother, looking into the fire. "But they're as full of mischief as an egg's full of meat. Was that Father I heard?"

126

No, it was only the wind howling into the chimney. Neither Mother nor Brigid felt like lighting the wall lamp. They crouched by the chimney and listened for the sound of two high voices and four small feet. The firelight threw huge queer-looking shadows against the walls like black ghosts and Brigid shut her eyes not to see them. All sorts of fantastic fears ran through her head. She thought of wild gypsies stealing her brothers, of wicked fairies luring them into swamps, of a miserable death down a precipice into the sea. She remembered the blood-red toadstool which she had seen in the woods the day before, and it seemed to grow bigger and bigger until it blotted out the sky. Then it vanished and all she saw was a big spider, rubbing his hairy legs and leering at her from the middle of a gigantic web, and saying: "Come on in, me sweet colleen." It was the voice of her mother that roused her.

"There they are!" It turned out to be only Father and Michael, who came to tell that the twins had not been seen by any of their neighbors. Father had grown anxious himself now and Michael's face was as white as a sheet. Mother fell back on her chair and moaned, covering her face with her hands.

"We'll have to notify the police," said Father. "Maybe they . . ." But he couldn't speak and turned away to hide his emotion. Pools gathered on the flagstones as the water dripped from his and Michael's clothes.

"What's that?" cried Brigid suddenly. "Did ye hear someone?" They all listened and as soon as Michael opened the door, Bran jumped into the kitchen, barking and spraying drops of water about the room as he shook himself dry.

"Bran! Where did ye leave the twins, boy?" No Francie and Liam followed him in, nor were they anywhere to be seen.

"There must have been an accident!" cried Mother, wringing her hands. Bran barked, and ran to the door and back, pulling at Michael's coat, as though asking him to follow. Mother took her shawl from the peg but Father restrained her.

"Be easy," he said. "It's a cold you're asking for if ye go out in this weather, and who'll be here then with blankets and hot tea to warm us when we come back? Sit down now, and everything will be all right." There was no help for it; Mother had to obey. But Brigid would not be left behind to dream of mushrooms and spiders. She put on her coat and followed Father and Michael into the darkness where the rain streamed into their faces and the wind tore at their clothes, flapping Brigid's skirts against her legs. She cowered as a streak of lightning flashed out, followed by a barking thunderclap. Father put out his hand and drew her arm through his. The touch comforted Brigid, so she walked on bravely.

Father carried a lantern that shed a pale ring of light, revealing a shimmering curtain of rain and little else. It would have been hard to follow Bran if he had not run back continually and barked loudly. It was difficult even so, for the dog had no idea of taking an easy road. He led them across fields, through hedges, over slippery stones and babbling streams and tall, stiff bracken. Luckily, Father's sprained ankle had recovered completely by this time. He and the children struggled on bravely, calling from time to time: "Francie! Liam!" and wondering with beating hearts whether they would find them dead or alive.

"Listen," said Michael suddenly. "I think I heard something. . . ." A faint high sound reached them through the roar of the storm—a sound as of fairies singing. Bran barked gaily, crashing forward through the bracken. When the others followed, they fancied they recognized the voices of the twins and they gave a sigh of relief. Alive, anyhow. Yes, both the rascals were singing with trembling voices:

> "Bold and undaunted, no cowards were they,
> There's as good blood as ever in Ireland today."

The flash of the lantern revealed two very wet, very frightened, very weary little boys sitting huddled under a gorse bush. One of them jumped up with a yell of delight, throwing himself upon his father whilst the other stretched out his arms and cried: "It's me foot! I can't walk!" Poor Francie! Father picked him up carefully and wrapped him in one of Mother's homespun blankets which he had brought.

"I'll have to carry him," he said. "You take the lantern, Michael. Are ye able to foot it, Liam?" Liam nodded. Father had some difficulty in finding his way back, but Bran, who was frantic with delight at having been able to aid his little masters, helped to show him the road and once on it they were as good as home.

The storm was drifting off, the thunder had ceased and the rain no longer poured down so fast. Mother had been watching for her darlings and came to meet them, pressing them both to her heart. She was very concerned about Francie's foot for Father told her he had suffered a great deal during the walk, though he had been too brave to cry out.

"It is all swollen," she said, taking off Francie's wet shoes. "Don't ye go hopping about on it now! Ye know how the doctor does be telling you to take it easy. Here, darling, Mother'll help you." She bathed the swollen,

misshapen foot in hot water. "It's getting worse; I wish I could send him to Dublin," she said with a sigh. "Whatever made ye go so far when the doctor told ye not to?"

"We were following the English," Liam explained. "I thought meself we ought to be going back but Francie said it'd be deserting the army. An' then it started to rain an' we ran an' we could hear the guns of the English soldiers boom, an' they firing at us that ye could see it up in the skies, an' then Francie couldn't go on."

"No," said Francie. "I couldn't walk any more for a great big bullet was after hitting me!"

"He said it was a bullet, but I knew it was his foot," explained Liam. "I couldn't be leaving him all alone to be caught by the enemy, could I now, Mother? So we had to hide ourselves like Gorrane did, an' the rain came down, an' the thunder boomed and boomed, an' Francie said it was the end of the world. Is there an end to the world, Mother?"

"Me poor laddies," whispered Mother, kissing her twins. "What happened then?"

"We sent Bran home," said Francie. "I told him how it was, an' he understood, didn't ye, boy-o?" Francie stroked Bran's head. It was true; they had forgotten the real hero of the adventure and Bran had the time of his life the way he was praised and petted and fed with Brigid's best scones.

"Maybe it is well to have a dog with the children," said Mother, preparing some nice hot bread and milk for the hungry twins.

"Maybe so," Father agreed.

"May we keep him, for sure?" asked Michael joyfully. Father and Mother nodded.

"Then I don't mind me foot," cried Francie sighing with contentment, and Liam and Brigid clapped their hands.

When the children had been fed, dried, and warmed, they were all tucked into bed, where they went to sleep at once except for Francie, who tossed about a long time, kept awake by the pain in his foot.

SEVEN

Paddy the Piper

ON MONDAY morning Francie's foot felt a little better; he could limp about. Mother wanted him to stay home from school and rest his foot, but Francie was so unhappy at the idea of being left behind that Mother allowed him to go, thinking that he would stay quieter on the school bench than anywhere else.

"You explain what happened to the teacher" she told Michael. "Ask her to keep him quiet."

"Faith, I will," said Michael. "But I'm afraid it can't be done." Little did he know Miss Reilly's resourcefulness. When Michael had told her what Mother wanted, she nodded and said she would think of something to keep him off his legs.

"We were lost yesterday" said Liam, after the twins had given her the Irish greeting.

135

"Lost, were you?" asked the teacher. "But you were found again, I see."

Frank and Liam both nodded.

"It was a good thing too," said Liam. "Francie, he couldn't walk at all, at all, an' we were near kilt with the hunger an' the thunder growling in the skies. Were you ever alone in a thunderstorm, Miss Reilly?"

"I was, once," the teacher admitted. "And I had to pray hard to keep up my courage."

"It's singing we were," said Francie. "But then, we are men. Girls do be more frightened at times."

Miss Reilly smiled. "Well, men," she said, "go to your places now and we'll do our lessons." Francie and Liam tried hard to keep their minds on the Irish alphabet that morning, but they would turn round occasionally to talk to the neighbors, who were thrilled to hear of their adventures. Once Francie made such a good imitation of a clap of thunder that the teacher decided this was her chance to combine discipline and care for his health.

"You're a bold boy," she said. "Now I won't allow ye to join the games at lunch time. You're to sit on a chair in the yard until I come to fetch ye." Poor Francie did not like that at all. He loved nothing so much as to be running around after a ball and holding his own in spite of his deformed foot. Still, it would be rather interesting to be punished. The other boys were looking at him with awe, which was a comfort. Sure enough, when the bell rang for recess, Francie was put on a chair in front of the school with his lunch on his lap, whilst the other children went to play in the field. Liam begged Miss Reilly to be allowed to keep his brother company.

"Sure an' I was as bold meself," he said wistfully. "I did the lightning an it was just Francie's luck he got the thunder." But Miss Reilly, though she laughed, was not to be mollified.

"Ye'll be getting into scrapes and be running around if I leave ye together," she said. "Let him stay by himself. It won't do him a bit of harm." So Liam, with a look of heartfelt sympathy at his brother, went to join the others.

Francie felt a bit awkward at first, with everyone staring at him, knowing that he was being punished. Then again, wasn't it rather glorious to be singled out in this manner? Wasn't he an extaordinary boy altogether to be punished like this? He took heart and began to munch his bread. The crumbs that dropped to the ground were noticed by a sparrow, who was hopping around in search of food. The sparrow immediately gobbled them up and twittered to his friends in the trees that he had found something good. A few more sparrows came fluttering along and Francie threw them bits of his bread, watching with interest their greedy delight. This was seen by a couple of crows, who were perching on the roof of the schoolhouse.

"Why should these common fellows be getting it all?" they said to each other, and swooped down to take their share. This aroused the jealousy of some tame pigeons, who joined the party hastily, followed by a few starlings and finches.

Soon Francie was surrounded by the creatures. Rising to his feet he offered all his bread to the birds that came flying from every direction to pick up the crumbs. Some hopped over his feet, in their haste to get the biggest bits, and a couple of bold starlings even tried to peck at the bread in his hands. Others alighted on his arms and shoulders in hopes of being specially favored. Francie stood in the midst of it all with bated breath, scarcely daring to move.

"They love me," he whispered to himself. "They know I won't do them any harm." His eyes shone with tenderness. When the school bell rang and the others came back from the field they stood still with surprise as they saw the little fellow and his birds. At their approach the creatures took alarm and soared away with great whirring of wings. Francie heaved a deep sigh and stood for a moment, thinking to himself. Then he ran to his teacher, completely forgetting that he was in disgrace.

"Did ye see that?" he cried. "Wasn't I just like Saint Francis?" There was a smile on Miss Reilly's face as she bent over to kiss the culprit.

"As often as you are kind and good to others you will be like Saint Francis," she whispered.

Miss Reilly had made Francie keep quiet, yet his foot was still quite painful, and Mother had to treat it when he came home. Liam stood by and watched as Mother bathed Francie's foot.

"Will I always have a bad foot, Mother?" asked the little boy wistfully. Mother sighed.

"The doctor says it can be mended," she said. "But it'll take a deal of time and money and it may hurt."

"Oh, Mother, I'll be brave. Sure, I never cry now, do I? Couldn't I be mended so that I can run fast and beat Shamus McCarthy at hurling?"

"Och, Francie, me darling, if I had the money I'd have sent ye long ago, but ye know how it is. Whenever I've saved a little, something is sure to happen and swallow it up."

Francie gave a deep sigh. "Can I be a great man, Mother, as great as Cuchulinn, an' have a lame foot anyway?" he asked.

Mother embraced him fondly. "Surely, greatness comes

141

from the brains and the heart, not from the feet, me boy," she whispered. "There's no reason why we shouldn't be proud of ye some day!"

Francie heaved another sigh. "Well," he said, "I'll offer it up. I know I will never beat Shamus McCarthy at hurling, but I don't care."

"That's me brave boy," said Mother.

As soon as school was over Brigid and Michael started off to their secret cave with Bran. Michael had put a stump of candle and a few matches in his pocket before leaving home that morning; he wanted to explore the cave further and see what it looked like inside. The children took great care to make sure they were not followed. They knew all would be up with their secret if even one of their schoolfellows found it out. They pretended to go in quite different directions at first and it took a long time before they reached the cave, what with stopping and listening and rubbing out their footprints. This time Brigid persuaded Bran to come into the cave with them, but the dog sniffed and whimpered and didn't seem happy at all.

"Maybe he is smelling ghosts," said Brigid with a shudder. "Ye don't think the cave is haunted, do ye?"

"It might be," muttered Michael. "People must have

been using the cave in olden times, and there is no knowing what may have happened to them." He lit the candle, and in the flickering light the cave looked spooky, with deep shadows dancing in recesses and corners. The children walked on until the roof of the cave dropped lower and they had to crawl on hands and knees. The candle flame smoked and flickered and wax dripped over onto Michael's fingers and onto the floor.

"Look at this!" said Brigid suddenly. Her bare knee had hit against a sharp object and she took it into the light to examine it. "It's a bone! It wouldn't be a man's bone, would it?" she asked, awestruck. It looked yellow with wormholes and spots on it. Michael couldn't tell.

"Ye never know," he said. "Somebody might have died here all right and then again it may only have been an animal, after all." Brigid dropped the thing with a shudder and they crawled on.

"Do ye really think people died here?" asked Brigid, who had pondered for a while in silence.

"I don't know—" said Michael slowly, as he poked his head into a crevice in the wall. It was dusty there and he found himself sneezing so he drew his head out again.

"Do you remember the writing on the wall? It sounds like someone might have been waiting here for someone else. Perhaps he starved to death!"

"Oh, please, Michael!"

"Well, maybe he was saved in the nick of time. Perhaps he found a rabbit and ate it, leaving the bones lying about."

"Rabbit bones are smaller"

"Well, a cow then, or an old horse."

"Ow! I've a cramp in me leg!" cried Brigid suddenly.

"That's from sitting here. Come along. Last time I left me knife sticking in the ground after carving our names and I want to look for it." Michael crawled through the cave with the lighted candle stump in his hand. "It must be somewhere," he said.

"Bran's looking too," remarked Brigid. The dog had been sniffing about the holes and corners for some time, scratching here and there and licking at the pebbles and stones he chanced to find. Now he suddenly started to dig into the ground with evident excitement, throwing up the sand between his hind legs.

"It wouldn't be down so far," said Michael. "I don't believe it's me knife he's looking for at all!" The children watched with interest as the dog dug deeper and deeper until his head disappeared into the hole.

"I'm afraid," whispered Brigid, clutching Michael's arm. "It wouldn't be more bones he's after, would it now?" The candlelight hovered over the jagged walls of

144

the cave and shadows moved in the corners. The children felt creepy and would have dragged Bran away but the dog had reached what he was after and, from the way he tugged, it seemed to be something heavy. Brigid held her hands tightly before her eyes but Michael's curiosity got the better of his fears and he peered into the hole Bran had dug.

"It's a box!" he cried. "Come and look, Biddy! It's a treasure, and we'll be rolling in riches all the days of our life!" He pulled at the handle as he spoke and he and Bran unearthed a flat box.

"How old it looks, doesn't it, Brigid? It may have been lying here for hundreds of years. It isn't locked properly. Give me a stick, Bridy; I'm thinking I'll be able to open it right here!"

"Why wouldn't ye use your knife?" asked Brigid slyly, holding her hand behind her back.

"Did ye find it?" cried Michael joyfully.

"I did then. Here it is." Brigid handed him his possession which had grown a little rustier but looked none the worse.

It was not difficult for Michael to pry open the lock which had grown weak with the years and the children eagerly lifted the squeaking lid. Inside they found a bundle covered with rolls and rolls of moldy, rotting linen

147

which they carefully removed. They were greatly disappointed when, at last, they came upon no pile of glittering gold but only layers of vellum, closely scribbled with ink, and loosely bound together.

"Oh, bah! Letters!" cried Brigid scornfully. "Old letters! Who wants them?"

"Whisht, ye never know," said Michael, fingering the leaves and trying to read the words on them. "It's very old Irish. I'd like to know what's written here. Perhaps teacher can help us. They may be old tales that no one has ever heard of!"

"Old tales?" cried Brigid, changing her mind. "I'd be willing to listen to them."

"You would surely," said her brother. "There may be secrets here that the world has been looking for, this long time. The secret of making gold perhaps, or of growing young again when you're old."

But Brigid shook her head. "It's not those we'll find there," she said. "Sure, and if the man who wrote all this knew how to make gold or to keep young, why would he have left the book buried in a cave? Isn't it more likely he'd be young now, and rolling in riches himself?"

Michael laughed at his bright sister, but would not relinquish the hope of some wonderful revelation.

"Listen!" whispered Brigid.

Out of the bushes close by came the sound of fairy music, or so it seemed. Gay silver notes trilled and tinkled swifter and merrier than a bird can sing, until Brigid's toes tingled for a dance. Bran cocked up his ears and darted into the bushes.

"I know who that is!" cried Brigid.

"So do I!" said Michael, taking up his box. The children followed Bran through the brushwood until they came to an open space where a little man sat with his back to a tree playing the flute. His clothes were so old they had lost their proper color and had taken a greenish tint as though covered with moss. His head had an elfin look with its pointed chin, round, apple-red cheeks, merry green eyes, and lock of sandy-colored hair. On his head he wore a pointed hat with round holes in it big enough for birds to fly in and out. All round him rabbits and squirrels sat listening to his music but at the approach of the children they fled.

"Paddy!" cried Brigid, running to him. "Is it yourself again! Will ye stay awhile now?"

"Well, well! If it isn't Brideen and Michael," said the little man, jumping up. "And a welcome sight ye are to a weary traveler. Isn't this the gypsies' dog, as fat and happy as ye please?" He stooped to pat Bran, who jumped up at him, trying to lick his face and hands all at once and waving an ecstatic tail.

"He was that," explained Michael. "But now he is ours and his name is Bran."

The children didn't have to ask how Paddy the Piper knew the dog, for Paddy was supposed to know every creature in Munster, Leinster, and Connacht. He was always going up and down the highways and byways of Ireland, taking hospitality where it was offered and playing the tune to dances and weddings until the very birds in the bushes knew the sound of his steps.

Michael told him the story of how he got Bran and Paddy nodded his approval.

"That was a good deed," he said. "Many's the time I've seen the poor creature beaten by those gypsies until ye could have turned him inside out. You'll be well rewarded; a dog repays a thousandfold any kindness ye show him. I've lived long enough in the world to know that."

"Will ye stay with us awhile now?" Brigid asked again, looking coaxingly into Paddy's merry face. His visits were so delightful and always much too short, she thought.

"I'd be glad to, if me bag didn't need refilling," said

150

Paddy, pointing to his knapsack, which usually contained many fascinating articles to be sold on the road. "I just came by to see me mother and bring her a present for her birthday. Then I'll be moving on to Bantrytown fair."

The children wanted to see the present so Paddy unstrapped his knapsack and took out a huge colored photograph of himself, taken at an American shop in Cork, as he told them proudly, where they knew how to do a man justice. Brigid secretly thought that the pink face with the smoothly slicked yellow hair that stared at her from the picture wasn't a bit like Paddy, but she didn't say so for she knew it would hurt his feelings.

Michael still clasped his old box and he suddenly felt that Paddy was the very person to solve the mystery of the writing.

"Do ye know the old Irish, Paddy?" he asked.

"I do then," said Paddy proudly. "I know it so well that I can be hearing the Irish words this minute that a man was only thinking to himself four hundred years ago!"

Michael had to ponder that.

"You must know it then," he said, greatly impressed. "Maybe you can tell us the secrets that are in this box." He handed it to the piper.

Paddy opened the lid and carefully lifted out the yellow sheets of vellum. His eyes grew rounder and rounder and as green as emeralds as they roved over the closely written pages.

"Where did ye find this?" he cried, and Michael had to tell all about the hidden cave and how Bran had dug the box up. Paddy listened silently, nodding his head now and then and laying a gnarled finger to his nose.

"This is a mighty discovery if it's not mistaken I am," he said, when Michael had finished his tale. "These are poems, children, the songs of many old bards, full of true Irish wisdom and music!" In his excitement he ran his long fingers through his hair till it stood on end. His hat had fallen off, but he didn't heed it for he was reading the poetry. Sometimes he declaimed bits in a loud voice but the Irish of the children was not good enough for them to appreciate the beauty. At last they longed heartily for Paddy to be done.

"This is a treasure," the little man said after a while with a deep sigh. "MacGeoghan must see this!"

"Who is MacGeoghan?" asked Brigid.

"MacGeoghan is a friend of mine who has a shop in Dublin where he sells only things that are so old that people have forgotten they were ever made until they see them in his window. He knows more about the times

154

before Cromwell than anyone in Ireland; he will tell me who wrote these poems."

"Will you take them away then?" asked Michael, who felt that he and Brigid owned them and didn't like to be deprived of their lucky find.

"I'll have to, if they're to be of any use to anyone," said Paddy. "Don't look so sad, boy, it's something much nicer than poems I'll be bringing you next time I come by, bless your heart! You may choose yourself what you'd like best, and you too, Brideen! These poems are too valuable to be left about, so trust your old friend Paddy, me darlings, and leave the box with him."

"Will ye bring me a new knife then, with seven blades?" asked Michael.

"And a fine doll with a smile on her face for me?" added Brigid. Paddy promised and carefully wrapped the box in a piece of paper, after which he wound yards of string around it and stuffed it into his knapsack.

"Now I'll never be lonesome on the road," he said with a smile. "It's scholars and poets I'll be carrying on me back!" He strapped the knapsack to his shoulders and settled his hat on his head again. "It's time I went on," he said. "Will you be keeping me company?"

"We will, surely!" cried the children, who were only too

delighted and hoped to get a story out of Paddy on the way. Paddy knew stories about the very stones of the road; he could pick them out of the past like plums out of a Christmas cake.

"Can ye tell us what was in the poems in your own words?" Brigid asked hopefully, when they were well on the road home.

Paddy smiled. "There are so many," he said. "They are all about Ireland, for they were written when Ireland grieved sorely. Ye know how we'd been fighting the English ever since Dermot, King of Leinster, brought them to this country like the traitor he was. Ah, bitterly have our people suffered these eight hundred years from poverty and persecution. There were times, under Queen Elizabeth and later, when Cromwell came over us like a scourge, that an Irishman's life was held cheaper than that of a rabbit by the roadside. The land was taken from him, the woods were cut down and sold, and he was driven up the bare mountains where he had to wring his living from the stones. The true Irish were allowed no learning, no religion, no poetry, no possessions, often not even food. Up in the wilds roamed the patriots with the love of liberty in their hearts, longing to save Ireland but helpless as flies whose wings have been plucked. Those were the times when the grass itself wept on the fertile plains of

Meath—wept that ye could see the long tears dripping in the morning."

"That was the dew," muttered Brigid, who had a practical mind.

"Ah, no, you're mistaken now," said Paddy, shaking his head sadly. "Ye would have known better had ye tasted the drops."

"Why?"

"It's salt they were," said Paddy softly.

"Oh!" Brigid thought awhile. "How do ye know?" she asked presently.

"That's what the poem tells us."

"What happened then, how did we throw off the English?" asked Michael, who didn't like the mournful part of Irish history.

"That's another story, and it took a long time. I meself fought in the last rising, as well ye know. Ye see, the Irish spirit was too strong for the English. They could ban it and beat it and tear out its tongue, but it was like a smoldering flame and it would break out again and again. At last some young poets declared a republic one Easter day when the Great War was on, and seized Dublin for a short time. I was meself a young volunteer then in De Valera's army, and I heard Patrick Pearse read the declaration on the postoffice steps. But the English had the city in flames the next day and most of the leaders of the new republic were arrested and shot. They had known when they started that they were doomed to die, but it was their sacrifice that gave us courage to begin our last fight. It is to those young heroes that we owe our self-government, our industries, our corn fields, and the teaching of Irish in our schools. We may be thankful surely." Paddy stared out over Bantry Bay with moist eyes.

Brigid and Michael were silent. They remembered that Paddy's three brothers had all been killed during the troubles, as well as his father, and they suddenly felt shy. Paddy soon turned with a smile and took his flute out of his pocket.

"Now we'll have done with memories," he said, "and think of the present only." He entered Glengarriff piping the merry music of a jig. The sound warned the villagers who was coming and doors were opened, heads popped out, and voices cried: "It's Paddy the Piper again, it's himself!" Dogs and children soon ran to welcome him and there were greetings wherever he passed. By the time he started up the hill Mrs. O'Flaherty had been warned of his coming and came rushing out to meet him, flinging her arms around his neck.

"Wait now," said Paddy, taking down his knapsack. "It's your birthday tomorrow and I haven't forgotten, Mother darling. Here's a present I brought you." He gave her the picture.

She was delighted with it and showed it to the children, who pretended, to please her, that it was the first time they set eyes on it.

"It's the image of you and it'll have a proud place on me chimney piece," she cried fondly. But, alas, another destiny awaited it. Clementine came out of the stable, curious to see what was up. She had a jealous disposition and, when she saw Paddy the Piper, an angry light came into her eyes. Sidling close to her mistress she looked over Mrs. O'Flaherty's elbow and saw Paddy's photograph in her hands. Suddenly her big tongue curled around it and she ran away with the picture in her mouth, wickedly flapping her tail. Mrs. O'Flaherty gave a wail of despair and ran after her pet, crying in her most wheedling voice:

"Clementine! Come here! Clementine! Come to your own mistress, darling! Clementine! Give it back to me, will ye!" As her temper mounted and Clementine remained hopelessly out of reach, running hither and thither with wicked glances at her mistress, her tone changed. "Will ye

come here, Clementine! Will ye listen to me! Ye wicked beast, will ye listen, ye old boldface! Come here, I tell ye. Come here, ye blackguard. Come this minute, ye sarpint, or I'll break every bone in your body!"

But though her mistress was breathless with running and shouting, Clementine had no mind to obey and bounded gleefully over the meadow. It was Paddy who finally cornered the creature only to see the last bit of paper disappear into her mouth. Poor Mrs. O'Flaherty burst into tears and would have beaten her pet if Paddy had not prevented it.

"Sure, I'll get ye another picture next time I come by," he said, taking his mother by the arm. "Don't fret yourself over a little thing like that but pour me a cup of tea for it's dying with thirst I am."

Mrs. O'Flaherty immediately bustled into the cottage to put on the kettle and her son followed on her heels whilst Brigid and Michael ran home, bursting to tell all their news.

EIGHT

A Picnic on the Island

FRANCIE and Liam adored Paddy the Piper. As soon as they awoke the next morning they were out of their beds and into their breeches, in the hope of meeting him. Paddy was so accustomed to be out in the open air that he never could stay long indoors and would be roaming about before the cocks crowed. Sure enough, there he was at the well, drawing water for his mother.

Francie gave a whoop and Paddy looked up.

"Is it Cuchulinn and Finn I'm seeing?" he cried, and went to meet them, a bucket in each hand. It was his joke to call the twins by the names of those ancient warriors. He said they had the same spirit entirely.

The twins hurled themselves at him; Liam nearly fell into one of the buckets and spilled half the water over him.

"Well, what have ye been doing since I came here last? Have ye been using the scissors again?" Paddy remembered ruefully the holes they had cut into his hat on the last occasion.

162

"If it's the same to you, I'd rather keep me other clothes the way they are, though the ventilation in me hat has been a great comfort on hot days!" The twins blushed. They remembered how angry Mother had been and how Paddy had pleaded for them, saying that it was holes he'd been pining for secretly ever since he got the hat.

"I'll give ye a new one as soon as I'm grown," Cuchulinn promised him. "I'm going to be a policeman."

"Well, you'll have to grow a lot then," Paddy remarked,

163

looking down at Francie. "I meself tried for that high honor and they told me no one under six feet would do."

"Do ye think they'd mind me foot?" asked Francie anxiously. Paddy's eyes softened.

"The greatest of men," he said, "were the men who had something wrong with them and conquered it. There was a poet once who could not write down his own poems because he was blind, and a musician who could not hear his own pieces because he was deaf. Far away in a country over the sea one day, a babe was born and it was so deformed that people around wanted to kill it in mercy. But the angels protected it and it grew into a saint of great wisdom whom all men flocked to see."

"It's a policeman I'll be," Francie argued stubbornly, not attracted by scholarship or saintliness.

"I, too," echoed Liam.

"Well, who knows?" Paddy agreed cheerfully. "Maybe you'll be holding me up yet and asking me, have I a license for walking the roads; and when I don't show one, ye'll be locking me up for not watching me steps and knocking the motorcars to smithereens."

The twins laughed heartily at this notion, but they didn't laugh long for Clementine poked her nose around the corner of Mrs. O'Flaherty's cottage and rolled her eyes. She was devoured with jealousy for Paddy and would try to butt him whenever he came near. This time she pranced along the road with threatening motions of her head and the twins fled with a scream, hiding themselves behind Paddy's back.

Paddy laughed. "Arra, policemen, ye're not afraid of a cow, are ye?"

"She may be a cow," said a timid voice behind his back, "but it's a bull's look she gave us!" Paddy grinned.

"Watch what I do to her," he said, taking a blowpipe from his pocket and stuffing a wad of paper into it. He blew up his cheeks, and the next minute the paper ball flew through the air, and landed on Clementine's nose. She sneezed and capered, shaking her head and squinting down to see if her nose was still there; then she jumped around and galloped off with a comical look of dismay, her tail in the air. The twins emerged cautiously from behind Paddy's back, gleefully watching the cow's flying heels while they made a show of helping to pick up the buckets.

"Your tea is wetted!" cried Mrs. O'Flaherty from the door of her cottage, the curlpapers still in her hair. "You'd better come in and have a sup!" Paddy's quick legs soon reached the door, but he wasn't allowed to go through. The twins had fastened themselves to him like leeches and would not let go.

165

"Ye'll not sneak away when we turn our backs?" they begged. "Ye'll not run off on us like ye did last time? Ye'll stay awhile?" Paddy laughed and drew his little friends into the kitchen.

"Here, Mother, here's two more wanting me to take the day off. What do you say to that now?"

Mrs. O'Flaherty planted her hands on her hips and regarded her son gravely. "I say it would be a shame for you to leave your old mother to have a birthday all by herself. It's not as if I had any other children." Her voice grew husky and she turned her head away. The twins made ready to run, for they hated to see a grownup crying, but Paddy gave his mother a kiss that sounded like a cork popping out of a bottle and she smiled again.

"Sure, and I wouldn't desert ye today, Mother!" he said. "Didn't I miss a grand wedding down at Kilgarvan only for the pleasure of being with ye! I have a plan that'll make a day of it yet, you'll see!" And he winked mysteriously. The twins were all agog to pry the secret out of him, but though he lured them on with sly grimaces and fascinating whispers they could get nothing out of him, and down the road they heard their mother calling them to breakfast, so they had to give up.

"Paddy is planning to do something today," Liam announced importantly, when two plates of stirabout had taken away his first hunger.

"What?" asked Michael eagerly. Liam looked at Francie, who returned his glance.

"I can't tell," he said.

"Ah, come along!"

"No, it's a secret."

"A fine secret it is when Paddy lets it out to the likes of you! It's boasting ye are!"

Liam looked hurt, and Francie said "Pooh!"

"Sure, he wouldn't share his secrets with little boys," Brigid remarked. "They don't know a thing." She watched out of the corners of her eyes, waiting for the twins to blurt out everything; but Francie was unmoved.

"Paddy knows we wouldn't tell," he said calmly, snatching another slice of bread. "Not if you pulled our nails out one by one, we wouldn't." He shut his mouth grimly. Mother put her hands to her ears.

"Bless the boy, where does he get those bloodthirsty ideas!"

"I don't get them anywhere," Francie said scornfully. "They come to me natural." His mother shivered and the others laughed.

"Well, I'm going to find out Paddy's secret!" cried Michael impatiently. "If he told it to them he'll tell it to me!" Dashing down his spoon he made for the door.

"Wait for me!" cried Brigid, hurriedly swallowing her tea. Of course the twins wouldn't be left behind, so the four of them burst into Mrs. O'Flaherty's kitchen and surprised Paddy in the act of devouring his last piece of bacon.

"They say you've told them a plan you have and they say it's a secret!" began Michael indignantly, pointing to Liam. Liam blushed but Paddy kept a grave face.

"That's right," he said. "That's about the size of it. I'm glad to hear they've not broken their promise." Liam's face lit up but mean old Paddy went on. "Now I've changed me mind and ye may let out me grand secret if ye like." The twins looked at each other and remained mute. Paddy took pity on them.

"Well, I see ye don't know how to begin," he said, laughing a little to one side of his mouth. "I know someone who'll be able to do it better. Mother!" He called and Mrs. O'Flaherty hurried from the bedroom, dressed in her Sunday-best. "Tell them the news, will ye?" Mrs. O'Flaherty's face beamed.

"We're to go on a picnic!" she said. "We'll be out for the day and all of you are welcome. I was just on me way to ask your mother."

"Hurray!" cried the children. The twins quite forgot they had pretended to know all the time and exulted openly.

Father and Mother O'Sullivan were delighted to accept the invitation. There was no work to be done that day that couldn't be done as well tomorrow, and it was long since they had been on a regular holiday. They were to go in Mr. O'Sullivan's boat, and row to one of the islands where they'd make a fire and roast potatoes and cook the fish they would catch. The day couldn't be finer and everyone felt in high spirits.

First the food and fishing tackle had to be packed and Brigid was instructed to wash the ears of the twins. Their howls mingled with the excited barking of Bran and the sad lowing of the poor cow Clementine, who had to be left behind, as she was inclined to get sick in a boat. Mrs. O'Flaherty hated leaving her and she went down to the Murphys' to ask them if they would keep an eye on her.

"Her heart'll be broke if she sees me go. She's that jealous of me son she'd eat him if she could, bless her heart," she explained. "If ye send someone around now and again to see if she's got something to drink and to speak a friendly word to her I'll be much obliged."

The Murphys promised, and so, with a lump in her

throat, Mrs. O'Flaherty parted from her pet. Clementine stuck her head out over the lower half of her stable door and mooed tragically when she saw the happy party go off without her. Three times her mistress turned to wave to her, then the bushes at the bend of the road swallowed her up. Clementine gave a sniff and settled down on the straw for a lonely chew.

Bran, of course, was allowed to come; he jumped, barked, romped, tailwaggled, and goggled his delight. He and the twins ran up and down the road whilst the others came behind slowly, laden with nets and oars and pans and packages.

Father's boat was beached in a small inlet of the bay, where pine trees soughed dolefully and brown weeds trailed down into the water from the pebbly shore. It was a nice roomy boat, and the packages and pans could be stowed away safely in a dry spot under the front seat. When they had all climbed in, Father and Paddy each took an oar and softly the boat glided between weed-laden stones and towering pines out into the bay. There the water surged more strongly, the boat rocked, and a breeze blew the locks of the children into their eyes.

"Mm! How the wind smells!" cried Brigid, sniffing up the snappy sea air and licking the salt from her lips. The

170

water sparkled in the sun, overhead seagulls screeched and circled darting down now and again to snatch up a fish, their wings cutting the air like silver scythes. Steadily the boat made its way, the waves gurgling and lapping against the bottom, the oars creaking and sighing as they swung to and fro. The morning light shone on the faces of the women, who sat back in their seats with contented smiles, glad to have a day off.

When they were well out into the bay, Father and Paddy put out the nets. While they worked, the twins fished in the water with their fingers, trying to catch pieces of floating seaweed, till their mother told them to leave off or they'd fall in. Bran behaved very well; he sat in a huddle in the middle of the boat and felt too unsafe to dare move a paw. When the nets were spread Paddy and Father took the oars up again and they rippled on.

At last the boat arrived at the largest island in the bay, where they moored it to a stone. They all scrambled out and the children ran around the island, exploring it and peeping around rocks whilst the men hauled up their catch. It wasn't a large haul, but there were enough mackerel for a good meal, and they set to cleaning them.

Meanwhile Brigid and Michael went looking for sticks to build a fire and the twins romped on the long, waving grass with Bran. Under a small, crooked, windswept tree where Mother built an oven, she and Mrs. O'Flaherty kept a fire of pine cones and straw until the children came back with armfuls of wood. Then the potatoes were washed and dropped into a pan of sea water, whilst Mother put on the kettle with fresh water she had brought for the tea. Meanwhile the children slipped down to the pebbly beach to bathe. It was such lovely warm weather that Mother made no objections, though she warned them not to stay too long in the water, and she called out to Paddy to keep an eye on them on account of the currents.

The water was too cold for the children to venture far; they preferred to race around in the surf, sending fountains of spray into the blue air; or they urged Bran to fetch a stick they'd thrown in, and watched him sneeze and snort as he dived through the billows to retrieve it. Their laughter rang out clearly, causing Mother and Mrs. O'Flaherty to smile to themselves as they laid out the tin plates and spread butter on thick slices of bread.

At last the men clambered up the rocky slope with the clean fish, and as soon as the seafood sputtered on the skillet its lovely smell coaxed the children out of the water. They slipped back into their clothes, with chattering teeth. Smoothing their wet locks, they ran to get

172

warm and flopped breathlessly down on the grass under the pine tree, where a delicious meal awaited them.

"Here's to me darling Mother and may she live long!" said Paddy, lifting up his mug of tea. The children promptly cheered, saying they wished that Mrs. O'Flaherty had a birthday every day.

"God forgive ye, then I'd be old too soon!" chuckled Mrs. O'Flaherty, whose face shone with pleasure. They all felt lazy after the good food, and stretched themselves full length on the grass.

"Will ye be staying long, Paddy?" asked Michael. Paddy gave his nose a rub until it shone like a berry.

"I'll have to be leaving tomorrow," he said, with a guilty glance at his mother. "I'm going to the fair in Bantry to fill up me bag and then I'll be taking the bus to Cork!"

"So ye're going to the fair, Paddy?" said Father, taking a puff at his pipe. "Faith, we'll be together then, I'm going there meself with some eggs."

"Oh, Father, take us with you!" begged the children. "We love the fair."

"Maybe I will and maybe I won't," promised Father. "Hold yer whisht now, for I want to talk to Paddy. What's the hurry on ye that ye're leaving us so soon?"

173

"It's the poems the children found," explained Paddy. "They're shouting to come out into the world. Is it meself will keep them prisoner after the long years of waiting they had, under the cold wet sand? Sure, ye can't blame me if me feet are itching to be on their way to Dublin."

"What do ye plan to do with them?" asked Father.

"Sell them, if I can," said Paddy briefly. "The money belongs to the children, of course, but I don't know if the poems will be worth anything. I'd be willing to pay for having them published; they seem that valuable to me."

"Would ye get money, real money for them?" asked Brigid excitedly. "And would it belong to us entirely?"

"Hush, hush!" said Paddy. "Don't you go fancying things now. There's too much good in the world that's certain, to go worrying about what isn't certain. It's the fine fish you're after eating that ye should be thinking about and the warm sun on your skin and all the lovely days that roll like apples into your lap."

"Bedad, you're right, Paddy," Father agreed, blowing out a cloud of smoke. "We do be thinking of what might happen when we ought to be thankful for the good we've got."

Mother nodded silently over her knitting, a slow smile coming and going on her face.

"Tell us a story, Paddy," begged Francie, who was getting

restless among all these sleepy people. Even Bran sat dozing near the fire and Liam had put his head in Mother's lap and looked as though he didn't want to get up ever.

"Yes, yes, do tell us a story!" the others echoed. Paddy was nothing loath. Accustomed to the open air he seemed to need as little rest as the wild animals.

"Here goes," he said, settling himself more comfortably and tilting his hat against the sun. "In the days long ago, before Saint Patrick banished the snakes, there were giants in Ireland so big that they could swallow an ox whole. They were strong but they were just like any other

175

body in their hearts. So when a Connemara giant, called Fergus McGrath, who was champion of all Ireland, heard of another, stronger giant in Donegal he grew pale with jealousy, just as you or I would. He was getting old and there had been no need for him to fight for such a long time that he had gotten out of practice.

" 'Must I fight this new giant and prove I am stronger?' he asked of his little wife, his voice quavering as he said it. His wife said nothing as she sat by the fire with her knitting. She knew he was not what he had been, but she didn't mind that. She set no store by muscular strength. 'What's strength to a woman's wit?' she'd say. She just sat and knitted and counted stitches till her husband stamped out of the house in a rage.

"Well, the other giant—Donal was his name—was like a young bull, bursting to test his mettle. He had heard of Fergus McGrath's fame and he said it was all put up. He didn't believe it.

" 'I'm going to find out meself if he'll stand up in a fight,' he said, and he meant it. When Fergus heard this he quaked so the house shook.

" 'Must I fight him?' he asked of his wife, but his wife kept on knitting and counting stitches. Suddenly there was a big bang on the door and when Fergus peeped through the window he saw a man twice the size of himself waiting to be let in.

" 'It's Donal!' he cried, running around in a circle like a dog that's mad. 'It's not meself that'll knock the likes of him down! Ochone! Me reputation is ruined!' And he burst into tears. Then his wife saw that she must put by her knitting. 'Go to bed,' she said, 'and don't say a word. Leave it all to me!' Before the visitor knocked the second time she had lifted the latch.

" 'How are ye, ma'am?' the giant said. 'I'm Donal O'Mahoney from Donegal.' He tugged at his forelock, for he didn't carry a hat and he had been taught manners by his mother. 'Is Fergus McGrath at home?'

" 'He is not,' said the missus. 'But you're welcome all the same and he may be in any minute now. Sit ye down and make yourself comfortable.' So Donal scraped his boots on the threshold and went in. 'What might you be wanting of himself now?' asked Mrs. McGrath. 'It's not often we have visitors in these parts.'

" 'Have ye never heard him speak of me?' asked Donal in a disappointed voice. Mrs. McGrath pretended to think deeply. She wrinkled her forehead.

" 'No,' she said, 'unless you be the man that promised to call for the old suit he's grown out of.'

" 'How can I be him?' cried Donal with flashing eyes,

pushing out his chest. 'Sure, ye can't have looked at me properly, ma'am, or ye wouldn't be saying such a thing.' Mrs. McGrath took up her knitting again and settled herself beside the fire.

" 'It is true,' she said, glancing at him. 'The old suit would not fit you; you're too narrow in the shoulders.' Donal snorted, but awe crept into his eyes.

" 'Well, if so, it's your husband'll find a smaller man can beat him.' Donal puffed himself up with pride until he was a formidable sight. Fergus peered through the curtains of the press-bed and groaned.

" 'What's that?' asked Donal, who had sharp ears. 'Did I hear a man's voice?'

" 'No,' said Mrs. McGrath, dropping a stitch. 'It's only me wee babe has the colic.'

" 'Oh!' And Donal sank back in his chair. 'Will your husband be here soon?' he asked.

" 'He will, so. He has only gone out to the woods to root out some trees,' she said and, as she noticed the rumbling of thunder in the distance, she put up a finger. 'Do ye hear them falling? He has the wood nearly plowed up now. He pulls the trees out like radishes. "Why don't you use a hatchet?" says I to him often and often. "What for," says he, "when this way is simpler and saves trouble in the end?" So I let him be; he must have his own way in everything.'

Mrs. McGrath shook her head. 'It's terrible to be wedded to a man with a temper,' she went on with a sigh.

"Donal's cheeks paled and he began to fidget on his chair. 'What's the matter?' asked Mrs. McGrath. 'Aren't ye comfortable? Come, take a cake. They're me husband's favorite.' She handed him a stale dog biscuit. Donal took a bite and broke two teeth.

" 'Thank ye,' said he, putting the biscuit down. 'I'm not fond of sweets.'

" 'I'm sorry to hear it,' said Mrs. McGrath. 'If I had known you were coming I'd have made you something heartier; but me husband likes soft food.'

" 'Do ye think he'll be here soon?' asked Donal hastily, with a timid glance at the door.

" 'He'll be here as soon as he has loaded the trees on his back,' said the missus. 'Come and have a look at me babe to while away the time. He's a bit puny; all his brothers were handsome fellows, but hc, bcing the last and a trifle sickly, he's not much to look at for a six months' child. Still, have a peep.' And she led her visitor to the bed where her husband was lying and pulled the covers from his terrified face. When Donal saw the huge bearded fellow and heard he was only a six months' infant, he put a hand to his head.

" 'If so, what'll the father be like!' he thought, and

179

terror came over him like a whirlwind. 'Don't let me keep ye any longer, ma'am!' he said to Mrs. McGrath. 'I don't think I'll wait for your husband after all!' and he ran to the door, stumbling over a pitchfork.

" 'Och! I'm sorry now,' murmured Mrs. McGrath picking it up. 'Me husband *will* leave his pocket combs lying about. . . .' Donal didn't listen. He ran out of the door and down the road and up hill and down hill all the way until he reached his mother's kitchen, where he fell gasping on a chair and asked for a glass of water. Fergus crawled cautiously out of his bed.

" 'Is he gone?' said he. His wife had taken up her knitting and paid no attention to him.

" 'What's strength to a woman's wit? ' she thought."

"Oh, Paddy, that's a lovely story!" cried Brigid. "I never heard that one before!" Paddy grinned and chewed some grass.

"It's very old and very Irish," he said. "It's the kind of story that is told from father to son around the firesides in the West and everyone changes it a little. Most of our stories come that way. They are not dead tales, lying forgotten in a book on a dusty shelf. No, they live on the tongues of people and they grow and change like all live things."

"But Fergus wasn't truly Irish," said Francie, who had listened wide-eyed. "He was a coward."

"We're all cowards," Paddy explained, "when we meet something that's too strong for us."

"I'm not!" said Francie, setting his jaw. The others laughed.

"Did Donal find out about Fergus later?" asked Liam.

"Oh, no," said Paddy, "Donal was so frightened, he never again put the tip of his nose outside Donegal, and Fergus remained champion till he died."

181

"I'm glad," sighed Liam.

Bran had finished his afternoon nap and barked impatiently. He tugged at Francie's shirt, his eyes begging for a rollicking romp. The twins were ready for it, for their legs felt prickly from sitting, and soon the dog and the little boys tumbled out of sight, their mother's warning ringing in their ears: "Don't go too near the water!"

The older people sat around and talked a little longer but Michael and Brigid wandered off to the shore, where they found mussels on the rocks. They gathered as many as Brigid's apron would hold and then they found a jellyfish dithering on the seaweed, with long rosy tentacles flopping in all directions and blue veins running across its glassy body. They poked it with a stick and turned it over, looking with interest at its belly. When the shadows began to slant long across the grass, they went back to the others. They found their mother and Mrs. O'Flaherty busy packing up.

"Here, you help carry these down to the boat," Mother told Michael as soon as she saw him, and she shoved a parcel into his arms. "It's time to go."

"What am I to do with these?" asked Brigid, showing the contents of her apron.

"Bless your heart, where did you find so many mussels? Put them in this basket; they'll make a fine soup tomorrow!" Michael was already scrambling down to the boat, but on his way he met Father and Paddy, who came running back, looking worried.

"Did ye play with the boat, Michael?" shouted Father. "What have ye done with it?"

"I didn't touch it," said Michael indignantly. "We've not been near the place. We were on the other side of the island all the time!"

"Well, it's gone," Paddy explained quietly. He stood in his shirtsleeves with his thumbs tucked in the armholes of his waistcoat. He had wound a string of seaweed round his hat and he looked so funny that Michael would have laughed, if the news had not been so terrible.

"Gone?" he stammered, looking at the place where the boat had been moored. Only strands of seaweed floated on the empty waves which caught the amber glow of the late sky. "Gone. . . ." He looked around helplessly. It suddenly dawned on him that they were on an island and that they couldn't get off unless they had a boat. Pictures of a clammy night spent in the open, frosty breezes nipping toes and fingers, and a pale, indifferent moon looking down on huddled prisoners, flashed through his mind. "But we must find it," he cried. "It can't have gone far."

"What's the matter?" asked Brigid, who had followed

him and was climbing the rocks with a load of pans that clattered at each movement.

"The boat is gone!" shouted Michael. "We've got to find it!" He put down his burden, and started running off like a goat, Paddy after him. Father chose the opposite direction and Brigid joined him, putting her small hand into his large hairy one.

"Perhaps the twins went out in it," she suggested. "I haven't seen them for a long while."

"Begob!" Father stood still and frowned. "Maybe you're right!" An anxious look wrinkled his face.

"Here, I must go to Mother and find out what happened to the lads." He turned about and leaped up the hill in great strides, Brigid clinging breathlessly to his coat. "Mother!" he shouted, as soon as they caught sight of the women under the tree. "Mother! Where are the twins?"

Mother came running to them. "The twins?" she gasped. "I thought they were with you. . . . I haven't had me eye on them since they went off with their dog, God preserve us. Has anything happened to them?" She looked around wildly.

"I fear they may have gone in the boat," said Father, his voice trembling. "It's disappeared."

184

"Oh, why, why didn't ye keep an eye on them!" cried Mother fiercely, turning on poor Brigid, who flushed scarlet, the tears welling up in her eyes.

"Didn't ye know the scamps would be up to mischief?" But when Brigid burst out weeping she kissed her hurriedly. "Hush, it's me own fault entirely. I'm their mother that suckled them and should have known better than to lift me eyes off them a minute. There, there, don't take on, Mother didn't mean it. Hush, there's no time to be lost, we must be up and after them for fear they'll . . ." Her voice trailed off, she dared not say the fearful word "drown."

Father was already pacing the island, holloing for the twins. A clump of pine trees hid the north part of the bay from view and he dashed through it. As soon as he reached the open he saw the boat rocking uncertainly in the distance, and in it two helpless little boys waved frantically to attract notice. Father didn't stop to think at all. He promptly threw off his coat and shoes and plunged into the surf, the salt stinging his eyes as he dived.

Paddy and Michael were just clambering around the bend when they saw him leap. "There is the boat!" cried Michael, who spotted it at once with his sharp young

185

eyes. "And it isn't empty, I notice," added Paddy grimly. "I know what your father is after now." He shed his waistcoat and shirt to plunge into the water himself. "You stay here," he cried out. "There are whirlpools about. Go and tell your mother." Off he went to help Father. Michael dashed through the pines, running breathlessly till he saw his mother.

"Mother! Hollo! Mother!" he cried. "We've seen the boat! The twins are in it and Father and Paddy are swimming to fetch them!"

"Where, where?" cried Mother, hurriedly scanning the horizon but unable to see the boat on account of the trees.

"Come here, I'll show you." Michael dragged his mother through the clump of pines, followed by Brigid and Mrs. O'Flaherty, who twisted her apron and prophesied all sorts of dreadful things.

"There! look!" Mother flopped down on a convenient rock with a sigh half of relief and half of concern. She watched the two men struggling on to reach the boat which rolled perilously with its precious cargo.

"Will they make it?" asked Brigid anxiously. It seemed to her that her father was about to drown and she gave a shriek every time his head dipped under.

"Oh! me son!" wailed Mrs. O'Flaherty, wringing her

hands. "The last one that's left to me—Oh! I'll see him perish afore me naked eyes! O Saint Patrick and Saint Brigid, protect us!" But Mother said nothing; her eyes were glued to the boat and her lips moved soundlessly. The boat seemed to be drifting off and one of the twins put out an oar in an effort to stop it. This clumsy movement nearly unbalanced the boat and Father shouted from the water between hoarse gasps: "Leave go! Sit still . . . double-eared donkeys!" The boy dropped the oar into the water and it drifted away.

"Now they won't be able to row back!" wailed Brigid.

"Hush!" whispered Michael. "Don't worry, Mother, more'n you can help. Father'll settle it. . . ." His eyes followed his father's valiant efforts with admiration. In the meantime Paddy had noticed the floating oar and, seeing that Father was well on his way to the boat, he swerved and struck out after the oar. Mrs. O'Flaherty was now convinced he would be lost. She gave up wailing and started to weep, rocking herself to and fro and wiping away her copious tears with the tip of her shawl.

At last Father reached the boat. After some heaving and trying, he managed to climb in. The watchers on the shore could see the twins cling to him joyously, though the distance was too great to carry their voices. A moment later Paddy arrived with the oar and clambered in too. Then the men rowed the boat back with long sure strokes; Mrs. O'Sullivan and Mrs. O'Flaherty fell into each other's arms with cries of relief; Michael and Brigid hurrayed at the top of their voices and waved with all their might. Soon the boat was close enough for them to hear Bran's excited barking and the unceasing chatter of the rescued twins.

"What made you do such a foolish thing after I had warned you not to be venturing near the water?" asked Mother of her youngest sprouts, when the boat had landed and everyone sat around a newly lit fire to get warm and dry again.

"Francie wanted to row," explained Liam. "He wanted to go around the island and explore."

"And then the sea would not leave hold of us," added his brother. "We didn't mean to go so far, but we couldn't get back. I think the fishes pulled us, or maybe the sea fairies did."

"No, there are currents around; you were caught in one of them," explained Father. Francie shook his head.

"They were no currents," he protested. "They were big, black monsters, and made a fountain, and then there was another fountain and another. Bran was frightened too. He barked at them, he did. Are there giants in the sea, Paddy?" he asked hopefully.

"Giants in the sea, me darling?" said Paddy, who sat so close to the fire that his toes got singed and clouds of steam fled from his soaked trousers. "Giants? 'Course there are. Why wouldn't there be? And they are specially fond of little boys like you! There are great big dragons down there, and when they sweep their tails it storms and the ships sink and fall right down their mouths and are snapped up like that." Paddy snapped his fingers.

"Arra, don't fill his head with nonsense," protested Father. "He's fanciful enough already. You saw porpoises, me lad. They come around in shoals and squirt water through their nostrils. They are big fish." Michael looked enviously at his brothers. He was a little sorry he hadn't thought of getting lost in the boat himself. Now that all had ended well it seemed a grand adventure. But the twins snuggled close to their mother.

"We thought we'd never get back," whispered Liam tremulously. "The sea growled and growled and looked so deep and dark and we shouted and shouted till we had no more noise here." He pointed to his throat. "And then there was a huge fish with prickles standing on his back. We saw him quite close with teeth like Father's woodsaw. He looked at us and well I knew he'd have liked to eat us, only he couldn't, so he swam away."

Father shuddered and Mother pressed her boys close to her heart.

"A shark!" muttered Paddy, his face blanched. "Holy saints!" They were all silent for a minute, thinking of the merciful escape, not only of the boys but also of the grown men, who might easily have been attacked by the monster. Only rarely did sharks venture into the bay, so neither of the men had suspected the danger they were in. Mrs. O'Flaherty began to weep again, but Paddy wouldn't have it.

"Thanks be to God we're all back safely and it's songs we should be singing, not spilling tears!" he cried. "I'll start with a ballad." So Paddy sang:

> "Clarence McFadden, he wanted to waltz
> But his feet weren't gaited that way.
> He went to a teacher who looked at his feet
> And added two pounds to his pay.
>
> One two three,
> Balance like me,
> You're quite a fairy but you have your faults,
> Your left foot is lazy
> Your right foot is crazy
> But don't be unaisy, I'll teach you to waltz."

Everyone joined in the chorus and laughed at the last

couplet, in which Clarence gets entangled in his partner's feet and they both tumble on the floor.

"Now we'll sing *our* song!" cried Francie, eager to win some applause. So the twins stood up in the firelight, clasped each other's hand, and sang in their piercing treble:

> "Dan Dan was a funny wee man,
> He washed his face in the frying pan,
> His hair was like a donkey's tail,
> And he combed it with his big toe nail."

After that they were hugged by the women, though goodness knows they had been naughty enough and didn't deserve to be made so much of!

The sun had dropped low; it was time to hurry home. The breeze had died and the water in the bay stood like pale glass and mirrored the purple islands, the feathery yellow clouds, and the slowly winging seagulls. Stuffing the picnic things back in their place under the front seat, they all climbed into the boat. As it slowly glided off in the evening stillness, Mrs. O'Flaherty and Mother sang the wistful song about the "Minstrel Boy." Their voices rang clear across the water and seemed to express the thankfulness with which their hearts ran over. The twins dropped asleep against their mother's lap, Bran whimpered a little and then settled down quietly, and the elder children trailed their fingers in the water with drowsy content. Creak, splash, went the oars, until the boat bumped against the pebbly shore. The lovely holiday had ended.

NINE

The Fair

THE next morning Father agreed to take Brigid and Michael with him when he went to sell eggs at the fair.

"But the twins will have to stay home," he said. "They'd only get lost on me." The little boys looked very disappointed and Mother pitied them. She motioned them to her and confided a secret to their ears.

"We'll have the grand party, all by ourselves, when the others are gone," she whispered. "I'll be baking a cake for you, with sugar on top, but don't say a word or Brigid and Michael will be jealous!" The twins nodded and watched with composure how Father packed his market basket, whilst Brigid and Michael put on their coats and hats. Bran was allowed to go. It was a lovely day, the best weather for a fair, with a shining sun and crisp breeze.

"The bus goes at eight and we mustn't miss it!" said Father.

Mother had just time to kiss them all goodby when Paddy's whistle sounded outside. Father hurried off, swallowing his last drop of tea, and Michael, Brigid, and Bran followed at his heels. Mother waved to them from the doorway and then she turned back, an arm around each twin. The lips of the little boys quivered, but Mother's magic soon had them smiling again.

The great red bus stood waiting at the foot of the hill. It was no longer new; a long life on the roads of Ireland had put dents into it, and one of the windows was broken, but what harm, as long as the wheels still turned? The driver leaned against the bus, talking to one of the passengers. Several women sat inside, trying to tuck baskets with turkeys and bags of potatoes under their legs.

Suddenly the driver blew a whistle; it was time to take seats. Father put his basket of eggs at the back of the bus and sat down beside it. Paddy and the children took the seat opposite, Bran at their feet. One after another, the marketgoers took their places, greeting each other heartily and exchanging the news of the day. Their baskets cluttered the floor and there was a strong smell of fish.

The driver stuck his head through the broken window.

"Does anyone know whether Widow Farrell is coming?" he asked. "I can't be waiting all day for her!"

"There she is!" cried a voice, as a fat woman, loaded

with paper packages, came panting up the road. Several men helped her into the bus, and even so three of her parcels clattered back into the road. Brigid jumped down to pick them up.

"Thank ye kindly," said the woman, settling herself contentedly.

With a loud explosion, and a roaring and rattling of machinery, the bus was set into motion. Brigid and Michael were thrilled. It wasn't often they rode in the bus, and it seemed to them like having wings. The road being bumpy, there was terrific rattling and jolting. Once they came down with such a bang that another window burst. Father was anxious for his eggs.

"What ails the driver?" he said crossly.

The farmer beside him chuckled.

"It's a race he's holding with the Ballybogan bus. They have a bet on who'll first pass the crossroads. It'll slow down presently."

Father took the basket of eggs on his lap. He was afraid the jolting would smash them, and as he planned to buy some chickens with the money they would bring him, he didn't look pleased. The children squealed with delight every time the bus leaped.

As they approached Bantrytown the road gradually became cluttered with carts and animals bound for the fair. No fear of the bus going too fast now, for it had to stop whenever a herd of sheep or bullocks blocked the road. Michael and Brigid loved to watch the excitement. The tooting of the impatient bus would mingle with the cries of the farmers, the barking of dogs, and the mooing of the cattle as they were whipped to the side of the road, where they stood huddled in a frenzy of fear, watching the motorbus splutter triumphantly past.

"Are we nearly there, Father?" asked Michael, fidgeting on his seat.

But he need not have asked, for the town rose into sight. They could see its gray houses and its steeple from afar. The bus did not venture into the narrow streets which were crowded to overflowing, but stopped before an inn where the driver could quench his thirst.

"Now for it!" said Paddy, settling the pack on his back and winking at the children. Bran jumped out happily; he set no store by busses and greatly preferred his own feet, which he used to advantage as soon as he had gained firm ground. Brigid and Michael helped their father lift down the heavy basket and soon the party stood amidst gay and hurrying crowds and wondered where to go next.

The regular marketplace, enclosed by narrow houses, was filled with carts and cattle. Horses, cows, and bullocks mingled in great confusion, the noise of their trampling and roaring rising into the air.

"Careful, children!" warned Father as they picked their way along the dirty street. "Watch your feet!" But the children had no attention to spare for their feet; they were far too interested in what went on around them. One man showed off his horse to a buyer and trotted it up and down in great style.

"What do ye think of that?" he asked proudly.

The buyer sniffed and spat tobacco on the cobbles.

"If ye hadn't told me it was a horse," he said, "I'd never have known it. I'll offer ye fifteen pounds for it."

"Fifteen pounds!" The owner of the horse rolled his eyes as though he were about to have a stroke. "I wouldn't sell half of him for that! Sure, it's not with the likes of you I'll be wasting me time." And he led the horse away with a great show of indignation until the buyer called him back to make a better offer.

Michael and Brigid would have enjoyed watching the horse sold, but Father pushed his way into a narrow street lined with handcarts and crates. Here smaller vendors called attention to their wares. Paddy nosed about looking for little knick-knacks to sell on the road. He bought some holy pictures and buttons and silver thimbles. Meanwhile the children listened to a tall dark man beside a cart full of old clothes, who was trying to sell a frockcoat much the worse for wear.

"Here's the greatest bargain of the fair!" he cried. "Won't it look elegant at a funeral when herself has run the iron over it? Ah! I see by yon man's nose that he's thinking of getting himself a wife! It's a coat he's pining for, no doubt, that'll put the young lady in the right frame of mind. Wouldn't a prince himself look well in this one, an' wouldn't a girl be proud to hang onto this sleeve in church?"

A little further on, a man stood on a soap box, wheedling the crowd into buying his medicines.

"Here ye've got a bottle of wonderwater that'll cure all the ills in your house!" he shouted hoarsely. "I got it straight from the fairies in the bog!"

Brigid and Michael felt it must be wonderful to own such a bottle and they were surprised that Father and Paddy took no notice. When they asked Paddy the reason, he winked and told them he always got it straight from the fairies himself.

"Three halfpence the bananas! Three halfpence the bananas!" cried an old woman wheeling a baby carriage filled with fruit.

"Two for a penny! Two for a penny!" A smell of spicy

applecake floated out of a tent where a young girl advertised her cuts of pastry.

Brigid and Michael sniffed hungrily, but they had no pennies and they knew it was too soon after breakfast to coax any out of Father.

"Can we look around a bit?" asked Brigid, when she saw Father settling himself in a corner with his basket.

"I'll take you!" said Paddy. "Fairs are the love of me life!" He grasped a child by each hand, Bran bounding after them with his tongue out.

Paddy wasn't like other grownups. He didn't hurry past all the interesting sights to linger long where there was naught to see.

He enjoyed the wonders of the fair as much as the children and he seemed to have a pocketful of pennies which he didn't mind parting with. That was lucky, because pennies would buy rides on the scarlet merry-go-round, and peeps at the two-headed calf, and tastes of the colored sweeties in the glass jar. In one tent pretty toys had been placed in a row, and if you could throw a ring around one it was yours. A gorgeous wax doll sat smiling at Brigid and bobbing her flaxen curls. For a penny she could buy ten rings, so Paddy put his hand into his everlasting pocket and Brigid had her ten rings. She held her breath till she was red in the face before she threw the first. Alas! It fell feebly at the showman's feet. Brigid twisted and turned and bit her tongue and tried her utmost, but the rings would not settle on the doll at all. Paddy was sorry for her and pressed a second penny into her hand. Just then, however, a blind beggar shuffled through the crowd rattling a tin box.

"For the mercy of God, will ye give something to a stone-blind man an' him without sight!" he cried hoarsely. Brigid thought how sad it must be never to see the sun and the trees and all the happy things of the earth.

"Sure, I don't need the doll," she thought to herself. "Amn't I well off the way I am?" She dropped the penny into the beggar's box.

"May the angels of God reward you!" cried the old man gratefully.

Michael tried his luck at the shooting range with a real rifle. Seven toy ducks swam in a basin of water at the back of the tent. If you shot one, it went under and you won a prize. Michael had learned to shoot well, and it was not long before he had earned a shining brown pipe.

"That'll be fine for Father!" he cried. "You don't smoke, do you, Paddy?" Paddy shook his head.

"When I'm a man I'll want me pipe," said Michael,

202

sticking the one he held into his mouth and pretending to puff out rings of smoke.

Paddy smiled.

"Don't be in a hurry," he said. "Ye don't know what ye have until ye miss it."

"What do I have then?" asked Michael.

"Ye have a clean nose, that can tell the difference between turf smoke and wood smoke, that can smell the dew on the grass and the salt of the sea on the breeze. I took to smoking for a while meself, and me nose got so clogged that I didn't know me mother was frying fish until she set the dish in front of me. Oh, no, I'd rather have the glory of God's good smells than a hundred pounds of tobaccy!"

That was a new idea to Michael, and he twisted the pipe thoughtfully between his fingers.

"Father smokes," he said at last, as the best argument he could find.

"Well, and so he may if he likes it," said Paddy generously. "Your father is a hardworking man, and it isn't Paddy would begrudge him his hearty pipeful at the fireside. Only, I'm saying ye don't know what ye have until ye miss it!"

"Where's Bran?" asked Brigid, who had lost sight of

the dog. Poor Bran had got weary of waiting at the heels of his master and mistress whilst they enjoyed themselves and had gone off on a trip of his own.

He had made friends with a proud Kerry Blue terrier, and a more companionable black poodle. The poodle and Bran had amused themselves by teasing the Kerry Blue until that aristocratic dog took offense and stalked away. Now Bran came leaping around a corner in answer to Michael's call.

"It is time to go back to your father," said Paddy. "He may be looking for us." He led the way across the market-square.

It was fuller even than when they had left it, and they had to dodge many a fretful bullock and prancing horse. They were picking their way among the shouting dealers when the angelus bells rang out from the old steeple.

A sudden hush fell over the town as farmers lifted their caps and women bent their shawled heads with moving lips. Paddy and the children joined in the prayers until the sound of bells had died away and the hum of buying and selling again filled the air.

"I see Father!" cried Michael. "He's after buying the chickens!"

True enough, there was Father, a basket in each hand.

"I sold all me eggs," he told them merrily. "And I got a wonderful bargain here, the best chickens ever we had."

"Look what I got for you, Father!" said Michael, handing him the pipe. "I won it meself at the shooting!"

Father felt proud and pleased, but he shook his head when he heard how Paddy had been spending his pennies.

"Ye shouldn't have done it," he protested. "It's little enough ye have yourself!"

"It's little enough I need," Paddy answered cheerfully. "When it's gone, here's a friend that'll bring me more." He patted his flute. "Sure, I'm the one enjoyed himself most, what with thinking I was a boy meself again and watching these fine children of yours enjoying the wonders of a fair. No more foolishness now." And Father had to leave off for Paddy would not be pitied.

"It's food we're all wanting," he said. So they went into a little tent where they seated themselves on a bench and ordered mugs of hot tea. Father unpacked the slices of bread and butter Mother had prepared that morning and found a bone for Bran in a brown bag.

"What time does your bus leave, Paddy?" asked Father after a large gulp of tea.

"One o'clock," said Paddy. The children had forgotten

Paddy would be leaving them and they begged him to come back soon.

"Don't forget the doll ye promised me!" said Brigid. "And the knife," added Michael.

Paddy smiled. "Don't be uneasy," he said. "I'll be standing in front of your nose before ye know it is me! Weeds don't wither!"

"Were you ever stolen by the fairies, Paddy?" asked Brigid curiously.

"Who, me?" asked Paddy, looking sidelong into her blue eyes. "Not that I know of."

"I thought you might have been. . . ." said Brigid slowly. "You're . . . not like Father, or . . . or Mr. Murphy. . . . You're like a fairy yourself—a good one, of course," she added hastily. Paddy burst into laughter that sounded like rain pattering on glass.

"I'm glad ye've a good opinion of me character anyway," he said. "I'll do me best to live up to it. But I'll have to be going now or I'll miss me bus."

"I'll take ye!" cried Michael. "And I!" said Brigid. "Or do ye want me to help you, Father?"

Her father shook his head and waved her off. "You two enjoy the fair," he said. "I'll meet ye at the pier at four; we're going back by ferry."

"That's fine!" cried Brigid and then she ran after Paddy and Michael, who had already started on their way. It was sad to part with Paddy, but he promised to be back soon with plenty of tales to tell and he pressed a penny into each grateful little fist as he boarded the bus. "Take heart!" he said. "The sun isn't down yet, and good things are waiting round the corner!" With a wink and a wave he disappeared inside just as the bus gave a lurch and started on its way. The children remained staring long after it had rounded the corner.

"What'll we do now?" they sighed, feeling as though all pleasure had left with Paddy. The sound of a drum attracted their attention and they saw a haggard gypsy woman, hung with beads and bracelets, beckon to them from the opening of her tent.

"Let me tell ye your fortunes, me darlings!" she wheedled, showing her black teeth. "It's an elegant fortune I can tell ye for a penny, and glad ye'll be to know it. There's good luck awaiting ye, I can see it by your noses! Your fortune for a penny! Your fortune for a penny!"

Brigid turned over her treasure and wondered whether she should accept the bargain. But Michael had got a glimpse of a rough bearded fellow at the back of the tent and he heard Bran growling in his throat.

210

"Don't go," he whispered. "I don't like the looks of those people. Come along, you'll get your good fortune if it's coming to you, whether you waste a penny on it or no. Here, Bran!" and he whistled to the dog. So they passed on, followed by the scowling glances of the gypsy woman.

"What'll we do then?" asked Brigid, weighing the penny in her hand as if it were a gold piece. It wasn't an easy thing to decide. Of course, such a fortune must not be squandered, nor could it be divided into different pleasures. One choice each was all it allowed them. Slowly they paced the gay market streets, a frown settling between their eyes. There were many dainties for the tongue—long spirals of barley sugar catching the sun like amber, jars with black bullseyes, sticky slabs of nougat, and tins and tins of home-made toffee. Then there were the tempting and mysterious tents, where big billboards announced the most miraculous wonders of the world.

"I'd *like* to see the two-headed calf," Michael said wistfully, looking at a monstrous picture.

"Arra, Paddy told us it wasn't worth it," Brigid reminded him. "It's all put up."

"How does he know?" sighed Michael, turning reluctantly away.

"Paddy knows more about fairs than . . . than the man in the moon," his sister said firmly. No, one penny was not lightly to be parted with. If it had been more they might have bought a hat for Mother. Such lovely hats lay spread out upon old sacks on the pavement. One had a feather on it which was almost whole and of a beautiful red. But no two pennies in the world could buy it. So that settled it.

Michael felt it hard to pass the shooting tent; he had enjoyed himself so much that morning, he would have liked to try it again, but then his penny would be gone. So with a last woeful look he decided to wait and see if something better didn't turn up. Nothing seemed good enough for their pennies and the longer they wandered the more difficult it became. At last Brigid found a way out.

"Michael," she said. "I'm thinking we'll be sorry if we spend that money for ourselves. We'll always be wondering why we didn't do something else with it. But if we each buy one of those grand colored balloons up there and give them to the twins, we won't be sorry!" Michael turned his penny over for the last time. Then he nodded.

"That's right," he said. "That's what we'll do. I had forgotten the little fellows. Yes, yes, that's what we'll do. You always think of the right thing, Bridy!" The two of

212

them hurried to the opposite side where the balloon vendor stood, but here another difficulty presented itself. The balloons cost two pence apiece. Brigid and Michael had set their hearts on one for each twin, and they could not decide to pool their money. They told the balloon seller all about it.

"It's for the twins," they explained. "We want them to have one each and two pennies is all we've got."

"Two pennies will buy you a nice large one," said the man, cocking his eye on them. Michael wavered, but Brigid stood firm.

"One penny each is plenty," she said. "They're only wind in a cat's belly." The man threw up his head and laughed.

"I'll tell ye what," he said. "I won't go down on me price—that's against me principles—but I'll sell ye one and I'll make a present of the other, to the young lady's pretty eyes." With an elegant bow he handed them two balloons. Brigid flushed at the compliment.

"I'm sorry I was rude," she faltered. "I shouldn't have said that about a cat's b . . ." But the man wouldn't let her finish.

"Sure, ye've made me laugh and that was the best thing could happen to me. If I don't have a laugh every day I don't digest me food and if I don't digest me food I don't laugh, so you've saved me life!" and, waving his balloons at them, he turned on his heels to look for other customers.

"That *was* a nice man," murmured Brigid happily, eying her bobbing balloon. "Won't the twins be surprised?"

"Where's Bran?" asked Michael, who had stopped to fasten the string of his balloon to a buttonhole.

"Bran?" Brigid looked around with startled eyes. "What . . . what happened to him?" Michael whistled, but no dog bounded to his call. "I thought you were minding him!" said Brigid reproachfully. "He's your dog."

"He's your dog just as much and fine ye know it!" answered Michael. "It's you might have kept an eye on him."

"I was talking with the man," protested Brigid. "I can't do everything at once."

"Well, don't blame me. I was talking to the man too!" Michael said angrily.

"Well, he's gone now. We'd better be looking for him instead of fighting!" Brigid ran down the street, calling out Bran's name.

"I'll go the other way!" shouted Michael. But though the children searched streets and alleys and called till their throats felt dry, they found no Bran.

"It's no use," cried Brigid, meeting Michael again on

216

the marketplace and nearly upsetting a basket of apples in her hurry. "He's gone entirely," and she burst into tears.

"What's the matter, deary?" asked the woman who owned the apples. She sat on an empty basket huddled in her black hooded shawl with scarlet lining. "Are ye after losing something?"

Brigid rubbed the tears back into her eyes. "It's our dog," she said. "He's run off on us!"

"Don't you fret," the woman consoled her. "He'll be back presently. Dogs know their ways about; they've sharp noses. What kind of a dog might it be now?"

"A little black and white dog with a pointed head and floppy ears."

"My!" said the woman. "Wasn't he playing with me Dicky awhile ago?" And she called out: "Dicky! Dicky!"

A dirty black poodle scurried around the corner but no Bran followed.

"Thank ye kindly, ma'am," said Brigid. "I think we'd better go to the police." She ran off with Michael in search of the police station. They felt better when a smiling constable had written all Bran's charms into his notebook and promised to look out for him.

But they still hoped to find him before it was time to go and they felt terribly upset when all their efforts failed.

"Maybe the gypsies took him back," whispered Michael. "I saw a great bearded man at the fortune-teller's tent!"

It was past four when they made their way to the pier at last and their father stood looking out for them and scolded them for being late. They explained about Bran but they could scarcely make themselves heard through the rumbling and shouting as the ferry was being loaded.

"It can't be helped," Father said at last, when he understood. "We can't wait any longer." And he pushed the children on board the boat.

With a great rattling of chains and three blasts of the horn the boat moved off, just as Brigid saw a small black and white creature bounding up the pier.

"Bran!" she shrieked, stretching out her arms across the widening water. Michael came to her side in one leap and minged his cries with hers; but the chug chug of the steamer slowly and surely parted them from their pet.

Bran understood, and ran up and down the pier whining pitifully. Suddenly he gave a leap and plunged into the water, bravely breasting the waves in an attempt to reach the boat.

"He'll never do it!" cried Brigid, wringing her hands. "We're going too fast, he'll *drown!*"

But Michael had already run off to find his father. Presently all the passengers knew the story and were

218

watching the antics of Bran with great interest. Father persuaded the captain to lessen the speed and after a while the poor dog was safely hauled up on a rope ladder. The children would have taken him into their arms at once if Bran had not frightened them off by shaking a spray of cold water in all directions. Then he dived into Brigid's lap and let himself be petted. He ogled her and waved an eloquent little tail but he never could explain how he made up with the Kerry Blue and went visiting at his new friend's home until conscience told him to look for his little masters.

So the day ended happily after all, with Brigid and Michael huddled in the stern of the boat, their pet between them, and all watching the foam of the wake dwindling in the distance.

The salt breeze played with their hair, set the balloons dancing on their strings, and dried the wet fur of Bran. The sun dropped down behind the purple mountains, leaving a honey-colored sky to welcome the first stars. The silent sea lapped softly against the sides of the boat, and gulls, like guardian angels, winged around with eerie cries. Soon they were among the green and rocky islands of Glengarriff harbor, where brown weeds trailed down into the silver water. The children could see the woods in the distance and even the roof of their home, peeping among the green leaves. The boat jolted ashore and the chains rattled as the gangway fell.

When Father and the children climbed up the road, they saw the twins on the lookout. Michael and Brigid waved to them and Bran barked lustily.

"Here, this is for you," said Brigid, shoving the string of her purple balloon into Liam's hand.

"This is for you," added Michael, presenting his red one to Francie. Looking into the blissful faces of the twins they certainly did not regret their pennies!

TEN

Paddy Returns

THE last leaves shriveled and fell, the lazy sun peered faintly through wet mists, and silver frost lay over the fields in the mornings, but still Paddy hadn't come back.

The children looked for him every day and wearied Mother with their impatience.

"What can be keeping him?" they wondered. "He promised to be here soon!"

Mother sat knitting woolen mufflers that would keep the cold rain from dribbling down their backs.

"He'll come," she said, "in his own good time."

The children hurried from school these days, for raw winds came blustering over the mountains and the roads were filled with puddles. They loved the fireside with its glowing coals of peat and liked to crouch in front of it to roast apples and nuts and forget the discomforts of the season.

One evening they were all gathered together. Mother had done her day's work and was taking her ease in the chimney corner, listening to the rain that pattered on roof and windows; Father had filled his best pipe—the one Michael had given him—and was stretching out his legs to the warmth of the fire; the children were grouped around him. Suddenly they were all startled by a loud knock at the door.

"Who might that be?" cried Mother.

Michael jumped up to let the stranger in, who turned out to be none else than Paddy himself, the water dripping from his hat and breeches onto the flagstones.

Cries of pleasure greeted him; Bran barked and the twins clung to his hands so that he had to shake one off before he could greet Mother properly. Father cleared a chair for him near the fire and Mother carried away his wet jacket and hat and made him take off his shoes.

"Sit down and make yourself comfortable," she said. "The children left me no peace the way they were asking for you. Sure, you're a welcome sight to all of us!"

Paddy gratefully took the seat that was offered him and stretched out his hands to the blaze, rubbing the numbness out of them.

"I've been walking all day in the streaming water," he said, "until I wondered would I drown or just melt away like sugar. It's a comfort to be near a fire again."

"Where did you come from?" asked Father, puffing out a cloud of smoke.

"I footed it from Cork the last three days, for I'd no money left to ride the bus. But I bear good tidings for all of you." His friendly face turned from Father to Mother, who was pouring hot water on fresh tea leaves, to Brigid hugging her shapeless doll, to Francie and Liam cracking nuts at his feet, and to Michael hanging over his father's chair.

The children were bursting to hear what he had brought for them, but they felt it would be bad manners to ask and so they kept silent, throwing shy glances at the knapsack on the floor.

"Well, let us hear it and don't be keeping us in suspense," said Mother, handing Paddy his cup. "Good news won't keep!"

Paddy chuckled.

"First I have to fortify myself," he said, and quickly drank his tea.

"That's better. Now hand me that bag!"

Four pairs of eyes lit up as he started to open his knapsack.

"Wasn't it a knife I promised you?" he asked Michael.

A vigorous nod was his answer, at which he produced the most wonderful knife that ever was made, with corkscrew and tin opener, as well as six sharp blades. Michael flushed with pleasure and could scarcely stammer out a shy "Thank ye" in his hurry to inspect the treasure.

"And here is a doll for me lady Brideen," added Paddy. "I couldn't get a real store one—they are too hard on my pennies—and, surely, an Irish girl doesn't want a foreign-made doll! So I carved ye one with me own hands, and a friend of mine who is handy with her needle made the clothes. I hope now ye'll like it." Paddy pulled out of his bag a creature that surpassed all Brigid's dreams.

Paddy was an artist as well as a poet. With skillful hands he had whittled the body and limbs out of cherry-wood, joining them with screws. But the head was the most wonderful part for he had carved it into a likeness of Brigid herself, and he had painted the face a lovely creamy color with pink cheeks and scarlet lips and large

gray eyes fringed with lashes. Red-gold curls of silk covered the back of the head and fell down in ringlets.

This beautiful creature was dressed in red petticoats, a black shawl round her shoulders. Her feet were left bare and she had a blue apron tied around the waist.

"Is that for me?" whispered Brigid, stretching out her arms. "Oh . . . isn't she a darling! Look, Mother! Look!

Father! See what Paddy made for me! Oh, Paddy!" And she was on the piper's knee in a twinkling, throwing her arms around him and planting a kiss on his nose.

Everyone wanted to see the doll. Mother admired the cut of the clothes; the twins wanted to find out could the legs and arms move; Michael, who didn't like dolls, said that this one wasn't bad at all; and Father exclaimed at the beautiful carving of the face.

Then Brigid would not have her doll handled any more. "Can't ye see she's a stranger here and doesn't want us all to be gaping at her?" she said, tucking the doll well into its shawl and softly rocking it to sleep. "It's Patricia I'll call her, after you, Paddy!" she whispered with shining eyes.

Paddy's face was bright with pleasure. He had enjoyed the work and he enjoyed Brigid's delight even more. He felt someone pull his sleeve and a little voice at his elbow asked timidly: "Didn't ye bring anything at all for us?"

"That's true, I was nearly forgetting ye!" cried Paddy, hastily diving back into his bag.

He brought out two little bows of aspenwood, cut with his own hand and tied with string. Each bow had three arrows belonging to it, made of reeds and goosefeathers.

"Now see if ye can learn to be as great hunters and warriors as Cuchulinn and Finn," he whispered, hanging the bows around the twins' shoulders.

"Can I really learn to shoot with it?" asked Francie, cocking an arrow.

"I'll teach ye," Paddy promised. "But don't try here,"— he held out a restraining hand—"or ye'll knock all the delft off the dresser!" He had caught Mother's anxious glance at her crockery.

"Lay down the bows now and come and sit on me knees—the best of me news is yet to come." Paddy pulled Liam onto his lap. Francie sat down at his feet beside Bran; Father and Mother dragged their chairs closer to the fire; and Michael and Brigid shared the bench, grinning expectantly.

"Ye know how I went to Dublin to see me friend MacGeoghan about the manuscript," Paddy began. "I found him in his shop and he greeted me gladly for we fought side by side in the days of the troubles.

" 'What is it ye want?' says he straightaway, knowing well by the look of me that I had an object in me visit.

" 'I come to show you something,' says I, 'and have your opinion on it.' So I take down me bag and get out the box of poems.

" 'Here it is,' says I. 'Take your time now and don't be in a hurry.'

"So he puts on his glasses and takes the box to the window, where he lifts the lid.

" 'Glory be to God,' says he, when his eyes fall on the old vellum covered with faded letters. 'Where did ye get hold of all this, Paddy?'

" 'I'll tell ye presently,' says I. 'First you say what ye think of it.'

"Well, he starts to read and, faith, ye could have heard a mouse wash his whiskers. Now and again he takes off his glasses and gives them a rub, or he wipes his eyes with the corner of his handkerchief. Once I saw a tear splash down, but ne'er a word did he say, but kept reading and reading until I was sorry I ever told him to take his time.

"At last he jumps up and clears his throat.

" 'Paddy,' he says, says he, 'Paddy.' Then he comes up to me and wrings me hand that I can feel it tingle in me toes. 'It's wonderful, boy, it's wonderful!' says he with a sniff. 'Where did ye get hold of it?'

"So I tell him the story of how two little friends of mine found it in an old cave, and he shakes his head at every word I say and goes back to the manuscript, stroking it with loving hands."

'These are genuine works of the seventeenth century,' says he at last. 'And the whole of Ireland will be rubbing its eyes in amazement when they are published. The poetry is the best of its kind ever I read and these children may be proud indeed for they've done a service to their country.' Yes, that's what he said: 'A service to their country.'" Paddy nodded at Michael and Brigid, who were blushing rosily.

"But Bran found it really," cried Michael, taking up the dog and hugging him. "He's the real hero!"

"Well, listen now, the best is yet to come," continued Paddy. "Me friend, he says to me: 'Paddy,' he says, 'I tell ye what, you bring this box to the National Library. It's against me own interest,' he says. 'But that's what ye ought to do.' So I took his advice and brought the poems to the National Library, where I saw the director himself and many learned doctors. As soon as I showed them the box, they were buzzing around it like flies around honey, looking at the poems through different glasses, testing the vellum and the ink, and fetching other old manuscripts to compare with it. At last they told me I'd better come back another day for this was too important to be settled in a hurry. Well, the long and the short of it is that they were very glad to take the poems and a great fuss has been made over them in the papers. But the best of it is that there is a reward offered to anyone who brings valuable books to the library and I have this minute in me pocket fifty pounds of good Irish money, which rightfully belongs to the finders of the manuscript." Paddy solemnly handed Michael a very bulky envelope.

There was a deep silence whilst the O'Sullivans were taking in this wonderful news. The only sounds in the kitchen were the ticking of the clock, the humming of the kettle, and the rustling of the rain.

"Is it really ours?" asked Michael at last, timidly fingering the envelope.

"Well, ye found the poems, didn't ye?" said Paddy.

"Bran did, really," whispered Brigid, throwing her arms around the dog. "He's an enchanted prince and he's made all our fortunes because we rescued him!"

"I wouldn't know what to do with so much money," muttered Michael. Then he bent over and whispered in Brigid's ear. Brigid nodded. "Mother," said Michael gravely, getting up and handing her the envelope. "This is too much altogether for me and Bridy to spend. Sure, many's the time we were longing to help you, so ye could have Francie's foot mended—isn't it so, Bridy?—and we couldn't. It's glad we are to be able now."

Mother had tears in her eyes and she pressed both her eldest born to her heart. "Thank ye, me darlings," she said simply, the firelight glowing on the soft happy curves of her face.

"Open it, Mother! Let's see the money!" cried Liam eagerly, and he clapped his hands when Mother showed him the crisp banknotes.

"Oh, look, Francie! Will there be any money left in the world at all, at all?" he gasped. "Will we live in a big house now an' ride in a car, an' will we have cake for breakfast every day?"

"Arra, no!" shouted Francie, poking his twin brother in the ribs. "It's traveling we'll be, surely, an' living on the road all day till we get to America an' there we'll buy whatever we fancy."

"But you *can't* go to America that way; you have to take a ship," argued Liam.

"Well, a ship then," said Francie, impatient with such trifles.

"Come here, darling," Mother cried, putting out a hand. Francie ran to her. "Do you understand what has happened?" she asked him seriously, lifting up his chin to look well into his rosy face. "Do ye remember what Mother told ye some time ago, that your foot could be made better if Mother had money to send you to Dublin?" Francie nodded, his gray eyes opening wide.

"Now Michael and Brigid have given me even more than I need and they want me to send you. Won't ye thank them for it?" Francie blushed, his eyes shone.

"Will I be made as well and as strong as Michael and Liam then?" he whispered. Mother nodded.

"That's what the doctor told me." Francie hid his face for a moment in Mother's lap. Then he went to Michael and solemnly shook his hand.

"Thank ye," he said in a trembling voice. But he flung both arms around Brigid's neck and just hugged her.

"Is Francie's foot going to be made well?" asked Liam. "Oh, that's great! Oh, Francie! Won't we have fun, an' maybe you'll beat us all at football! Hurray!" And Liam danced around the kitchen.

"Well," said Father. "Don't forget who took the trouble to take the poems to Dublin! Without him we might never have found out their value!"

"Oh, Paddy!" cried Brigid. "How could we forget him!" Paddy sat smiling in his chimney corner and didn't look the least bit hurt. He seemed more than ever like a good fairy, thought Brigid, the flames showing up his rugged features, the cherrylike cheeks, pointed ears, and cheerful nose. He sat there loving everyone and he looked more comfortable than the kettle singing on the chain.

"Don't you want some of the money, Paddy?" asked Michael timidly. "Ye've done it all for us . . . it seems a shame. . . ." But Paddy shook his head.

"Money is of no use to me," he said. "Money won't buy me the things I care for."

"What things?"

"Well . . . the swell of the sea and the sight of the gulls on the wing, the sweep of a road in front of me, the friendly faces greeting me at cottage doors, the kindness of the stars at night, and the wet nose of a dog pressed in me hand. . . . Money won't buy me the look in a mother's eye when she watches her child, nor will it make me flute play faster or me blood run stronger in me veins. . . . Money, me dear, means a lot, and then again it means nothing at all. It's all a matter of taste."

"But, Paddy, how can ye live without money?" asked Brigid.

"I don't," said Paddy. "Whenever I need some I've only to press the holes in me flute and it comes rolling into me lap."

"Oh! Let's see how ye do that?" asked Francie eagerly, but Paddy shook his head.

"This is not the right place," he said.

Father and Mother meanwhile had been making plans for spending the money.

"Let me see now," said Father. "Thirty pounds ought to be enough for Francie's foot, and there would still be twenty over. I know of a grand little cow I could get for that money from Farmer Flynn." A cow! A cow of their own! Mother thought of the pints of milk that would fill the children with health and strength. A cow! The children thought of the sound of a cowbell in their meadow, and warm sweet drinks straight from the udder. The grandeur of owning a cow! Only the twins objected.

"Not one like Clementine," they said. "Not one with horns." Father promised to get a meek one with soft, dark eyes and a velvety nose. The twins might ride on her when she went to the meadow.

"Oh, Paddy! It's the good news you brought us, and no mistake!" cried Mother. "How'll we ever thank you!"

"I'm thanked already," said Paddy, and he took his flute and began to play. First he played softly and dreamily, the silver notes falling into a hymn of thanksgiving. Then the tones swelled and grew swifter and swifter like a swirling river. They rose in bunches like grapes and burst and scattered down. Wilder and wilder went the music until the children were on their toes, dancing. Then the music settled into a hornpipe tune and Mother and Father jumped up and danced as though they were lass and lad. They formed reels and doubles whilst their feet twinkled so swiftly that you could hardly keep track of them. Francie and Liam did their level best to keep up with them and jigged like veterans.

The wind still howled down the chimney and the rain poured on the roof, stray drops falling into the fire with a hiss. In the kitchen it was all happiness and pattering feet, and at last the dancers dropped breathlessly back on their seats. Mother poured more water in the teapot and presently she and Brigid handed round the steaming cups with thick slabs of seedcake. Bran got a piece too.

"I never thought that dog would be anything but a worry," said Mother as she fed him. "Now I wouldn't part with him for anything."

"Nor would we," cried the children. "Darling Bran!"

Paddy got up, for his mother awaited him at his home. He had to promise to be back again the next day, otherwise the twins would not have let him go. Brigid made him kiss Patricia good-night and then she flung her arms around him herself. "Thank you, Paddy," she whispered. "Ye're made us *so* happy! The fairies couldn't have done it better!" Paddy grinned and went out into the rain.

"Well," said Father, yawning and stretching out his legs. "It turned out to be a lucky rabbit hole I fell into that day on the mountainside."

"Why, Father?" asked Michael.

"If I had not sprained me ankle, you two wouldn't have gone with the donkey, and the donkey wouldn't have run away, and ye wouldn't have got the dog. Then

Bran wouldn't have found the poems and we wouldn't have had the money. So ye see, it's not the big stones that build the castles!"

The children fell silent, thinking of the chain of incidents that ended in the good news of this day. The fire glowed softly and they could hear the rumble of the sea in the distance. Their eyelids grew heavy and their heads began to nod. Francie lay on his mother's lap and would have fallen asleep if she hadn't roused him.

"It's time for bed," she said, lighting the candle. "Come along, there's another day tomorrow!" And she led the way to the next room where she helped them to undress and tucked them all into bed. Then she blew out the candle. "*Go dtuggaigh dia o'ghe vaih ghuit,*" she said, which means "good-night!"

About the Author

Hilda van Stockum was born in Rotterdam, Holland, in 1908, daughter of a Dutch naval officer and an Irish-Dutch mother. She early on learned English from her mother, something which would stand her in good stead in the years ahead. Story-telling, art, fun and home-schooling (until age 10) enriched her young days. Her first plan was to become an artist. At age 16, having moved to Ireland with her family, she attended the School of Art in Dublin. She then returned to Holland to attend the Dutch Academy in Amsterdam. Writing frequent letters to her mother (between Holland and Ireland), she developed her descriptive skills which would blossom into a career of distinction: writing and illustrating children's books.

Once back in Ireland, Hilda van Stockum began her formal art career as a portrait painter, doing some book illustrating as well. It was during this time that she met and married American Ervin Ross Marlin in 1932. Shortly after, the acceptance of her first book, *A Day on Skates*, launched a long career of writing and illustrating books for children. After the Marlins moved to America, Hilda van Stockum wrote the three "Bantry Bay" books based on an actual family she had met, set in the countryside she knew and loved. For many years *Francie on the Run* was her personal favorite (a slot later shared with *The Borrowed House*). Empathy with children and an instinct for the importance of small things characterize these and all Miss van Stockum's works. She often used her own six children as models and sources of humorous anecdotes, including direct quotations. The Marlins settled eventually in England to be near three daughters and numerous grandchildren. Today Hilda van Stockum continues to wield a paintbrush that fully justifies the renown she earned in her *other* career as artist.

Francie on the Run
by Hilda van Stockum

This charming sequel to *The Cottage of Bantry Bay* picks up the O'Sullivan story immediately after Francie's successful operation in Dublin. Francie has missed all the fun of Christmas, St. Patrick's Day and Easter at home. He thinks it is high time to return to County Cork and his beloved family. Being a man of action, he considers it the most natural thing in the world to walk right on out of the hospital door. He has not the faintest idea about how to get home. He assumes that any train will take him to Bantry Bay; he promptly secures himself a seat on a train heading in the wrong direction. Thus begin the high adventures of one young Francis O'Sullivan. His forthright spirit brings light and laughter to all he meets in a whirlwind tour of the Emerald Isle.

Pegeen
by Hilda van Stockum

Young Pegeen was one of the many friends made by Francie in his trip around Ireland. Her Grannie has just now died. Pegeen sees no reason why she may not stay on in the small mountain cottage and fend for herself. However, neighbors, and even good Father Kelly, say her only relative who lives in New York will most likely send for her. Pegeen is heartbroken and Fr. Kelly himself wonders how this wild young thing will survive such a drastic change. Then Pegeen remembers Francie's promise to come for her in a white ship. With Father Kelly's help she writes to him. Happily, Mother O'Sullivan invites Pegeen to stay with them until things are settled with her uncle. No one, except perhaps Francie, is quite prepared for Pegeen's knack of turning the world up on end. Her spirit is a perfect match for his, but two such personalities in one small cottage on Bantry Bay have startling consequences—all of which add up to lively and unforgettable Irish tale.